ARETALOGY

Lineage of a God

Star Lore Publishing is a creation by André Consciência and Victoria Amadea Sulayman. Writers and practitioners of the esoteric sciences, it is their delight to deliver magic and art to you through Star Lore Publishing, specialized in magical fiction and occult books of time past.

Published by Star Lore Publishing
Vacaville, CA 95687
United States

StarLorePublishing.com

info@starlorepublishing.com

Design and layout by
André Consciência of Star Lore

Edited by
André Consciência
Victoria Amadea Sulayman

Acknowledgments

The versions of the story of Sinuhe in this book were adapted from the translations by Miriam Lichtheim. The version of Setne Khamwas I was adapted from the public domain version available at ib205.tripod.com. The central text in the book, the Aretalogy of Imhotep, was taken from Oxyrhynchus papyri vol. 11, pages 221-34, which is available in public domain from archive.org. Special thanks to Kim Ryholt for his summaries of texts such as "the Life of Imhotep" and to Garth Fowden for his help in locating the Aretalogy in the Oxyrhynchus Papyrii collection.

Foreword

Aretalogy, Lineage of a God, is unexpected. When we began Star Lore Publishing, it was just an idea. We were going to publish occult classics that we thought best deserved our attention, and wait to welcome fiction writers whose narratives touched the theme accordingly. Thanks to the noble and well-known Martin Faulks, Jack Kausch was introduced to us and, with him, the work at hand.

When I started reading it, I soon understood what it was that we were all about. Aretalogy was its incarnation, its voice, the tune of our song. This "Lineage of a God" was also the lineage from which we had just descended or to which we, luckily, had ascended.

Jack Kausch approaches the reader as a very talented storyteller but also as a philosopher masked as a fiction writer. He takes us to ancient Greece and Egypt and to the times of Alexandria, where we learn with masters of both cultures, schools of thought and traditions. Thus, grabbing the torch of Hermeticism by its flaming biforked root, we may yet unify with the one lineage of Hermes, Thoth, and Imhotep, or discover we are a part of it.

Aretalogy sounds less like a work of fiction than a work of sacred memory. Jack was kind enough to bring this reminiscence back to us all.

André Consciência

TABLE OF CONTENTS

PART ONE

Alexandria

The times have long come and gone since my soul sailed like a falcon in the blue above the Center Sea. That being said, my memory remains and now I, Psammethicus — although you may call me Psa. — return from the dead to write my story.

There are two forms of Time: one a snake devouring its tail, the other an arrow that targets Eternity. Within these forms we are bound as though by a mesh. If we move along the weft, we are lost to the warp, and so on. Yet wherever we choose to go the texture of the fabric remains the same.

My country has been lost to the wheel of time. Once it was called Aegypt, and it existed in the center of the world. To the West was the land of the Gods, to the East the birthplace of the Sun. These are coordinates, which means they are like scraps of torn fabric. It is about as good as saying "This End Up" or "This Way Is North" when all you have left of the map is a sliver. There is no way you will understand what I am saying unless you see it for yourself. So come with me.

"Hyginos," said Sumethres on the dock, casting another lot.

"What about him?" I said as I sat watching sails cut through wind on the harbor.

"Nasty piece of work." Sumethres moved three of his pebbles to another square. "Your move."

"I cannot say I care," I said. "I ignore him."

"How?" said Sumethres. "He lit a woman's cat on fire last week."

"Well. He's disgusting."

"Poo!" Sumethres threw his lot away and spit over the quay. "I do not understand you. First you go to that school and pretend to be Greek — they do not want to accept you, you practically have to beg them until uncle Manetho shows up, now you are sitting here letting this lunatic Hyginos shit all over everything that's sacred. What's the matter with you? It's such a massive insult."

3

"What should we do? Stone him to death? The King would have us at the tribunal to hang by our thumbs."

Sumethres crossed his eyes mockingly, like a child. "Hang us for practicing law?"

"For religious intolerance."

"Oh, I forgot. *'All Gods are images of the same God, having the same form, therefore up is down, left is right, Hermes is Thoth and Hephaestus is Ptah.'* HOW do you stomach it?"

"Well, that's just according to Herodotus," I said.

"Who?" said Sumethres.

"A Greek historian."

"What's History?" said Sumethres. "Come on, let's get lunch."

"Don't you want to finish this game?"

"It's your move, Psa! What's keeping you?"

I took a few more of his pebbles before the harbourmaster showed up. "What are you doing here? There's a ship from Tyre I need to dock here, and you're in the way. Come on, scram."

Sumethres gestured widely. "There are thirty berths along this side of the quay."

"And I'm using this one," the harbourmaster said. "I can make it harder for you as well."

"This is our country," I said. "We'll sit where we like."

The harbourmaster bent down and stuck his face into mine. "This is not your country. This is Alexandria."

Sumethres and I passed by the docks, near the ships beating the constant rhythm of loading and unloading, where foremen operated wooden cranes, or scribes marked on papyrus shipments of grain and metal, gesturing wildly at the workmen unloading amphorae, chests, crates. Later, this harbor would always say Harbor to me, as if it were the Harbor of the World — and it seemed then that it was, that its thousand painted sails contained the whole Ocean, or that its quays were the very World-Serpent, which encircled everything.

And yes, there was a Lighthouse.

"So." Sumethres said, "So." He gestured to his lips in that Egyptian way whereby a child says it wants to eat, or a grown man indicates he has something important to say. Thumb pointing inward.

"So to my friend Psammethicus, Hyginos is no bother. Apparently, my good friend Psa likes being beat up upon."

"Sumethres."

"He goes to their Musaion, he says to his new masters, 'Please am I a good dog yet? Please fix me...'"

"*Sumethres.*"

"What? You do not protest. What does Hyginos have to do?"

"I told you, I think it's disgusting."

"Oh, you do not know the half of it," Sumethres wheeled around to face me. "Hyginos is a baser metal than disgusting. That man is in an underground marriage with his own grandmother!"

"Gross."

"That guy is so insane, he would do anything. He already has done everything! Come on, what does he have to do? Hyginos would fuck a crocodile in the temple of the Crocodile God, my hand to God. He would embalm his own — "

"Alright! Fine, fine, I'm in, just stop. What's the plan?"

Sumethres howled and raised both his hands to the sky. "Praise the Sun! Psa, the man himself, schemes with the Ennead." He spun around, and whispered: "Meet me at the door of Unathes, a span after sundown. Be quick. Make sure you're not followed."

"Yeah, I know," I said.

"Good man," said Sumethres, grinning wide. "Now I'm off — got to find more recruits. Duty calls!" He sped off down one of the alleys along the quay, leaving me standing in the shadows of the ships and the workmen and the wooden cranes. I sighed. With Sumethres, there always had to be an ulterior motive.

I walked towards home, which in my case was a small cell in a royal dormitory of the Musaion. This was a prestigious berth. Some people (mostly Greeks) treated my membership in the Musaion as a kind of accident. It was an inconvenience that I had found my way there, and the only solution was to overlook my ethnicity entirely: all Gods are one. Others (mostly Egyptians) viewed it as a perversion, a scandal, a crime against nature, so they treated me as a foreigner or a fish-eater; that is, unclean. Still others (the Jews) could not care less about my ethnicity as far as scholarship was concerned, but if I ran into them drunk, after-dark at the ale house, they would note the cut of my toga and engage me in a debate about Moses which sometimes ended with knives being drawn, or at least insults exchanged.

I cannot say that I was popular, nor can I say with any real certainty what had possessed me to seek the position in the first place. It was as if I had been shunted through the gears of the celestial spheres, never intending any of it, somehow finding myself navigated to an unlikely and unenviable place.

In my childhood I grew up in the village. I learned to write from the local priests of the goddess Neith. I was just old enough to remember when King Ptolemy (the second) died. Everyone came together and carried the body of Osiris through the village. I remember the women wailing, tearing their dresses, clawing at their breasts. The men held burning incense in their hands and offered it to the God. I asked my mother why this was done. She said: "They are mourning the King in the Old Way."

This was the first time I learned that there was an Old Way and a New Way: that there had been a break in Time, and I was a part of it. In the years that followed I would fall into this rift and never get out, trapped always between two worlds that were about to rip me in two. Like Osiris, his body torn to pieces by his brother, Typhon. But there would be no kingship in the land of the dead for me. Only darkness.

For to die is to become Osiris, I hummed to myself as I walked. The rightful King forever returns.

At that moment I almost stumbled into a magician sitting by the side of the road, selling her wares. I tripped, caught myself, nearly lost a sandal.

"Well met, child of Sia," she said to me, a smile playing across her face.

"My heart does not dance with Sia, save before the court of the Gods."

"Nevertheless, you are one who loves wisdom." She spread her hands, as if beckoning me to inspect some of the small lazuli pendants of her purview. I ignored her.

"There is wisdom and there is Wisdom," I remarked. I was anxious to be gone but I could tell she was a holy person, and if I spoke against her I would speak against my heart - the first god she had invoked was Sia.

"Is not wisdom true no matter which race you are? Do not the Greeks call Thoth Hermes, and the Babylonians Shamash?"

"This is true. You speak like a philosopher."

"And where is the origin of philosophy? But I know nothing about this, I simply practice Heka."

"Do you have anything to sell me today?" I meant information. If I could get this mage to make some prophecy I could consider the matter settled, and please the Gods (who had clearly set this up), and be on my way home.

Not for the last time, I learned it was not so easy to outsmart them.

"You think you are immune to the Evil Eye?" She gestured to her charms again. "Even now this Hyginos makes war against you in his sleep. You think you are inculpable because of your status? He hates you on account of your race, and whatever your position is in the world of the conquerors you will always be an Egyptian, Psa." I recognized

10

then that it was not this woman speaking, but a God speaking through her.

"This is an Oracle? An Oracle posing as a magician on the street? And who are you, oh far-seeing-one — Isis?"

"In the time of the ancestors," the magus said, "The Gods conversed with man freely without the need of intermediaries; so it happens now through this one here. No Psammetichus, I am not Isis: you who write in the language of the barbarian invaders will find me your patron, willingly or no. I am the Goddess Seshat."

I was confused, and more than a little perturbed. "What message do you have for me, oh Lady of the Eternal Scroll?" I was doing my best to be polite here, a really bad idea to offend her now. But I could hardly remember any of the epithets of Seshat save that she inscribed the account of the years in the palm-leaf of Thoth, which emerged from the Ogdoad.

She laughed. Of course, I could not hide this from her. "I have given it you. Be on your guard against treachery. You think that you can ride the wings of Mind and avoid all conflicts. But that is not your fate: you are a man, and an Egyptian at that. You have not begun to understand your role. You must pick a side." A shadow passed over the mage's eyes. She was herself again. "Would you like to buy a charm?"

Of course I did, I am no fool. I put a wadj on a string around my neck — *You think you are immune to the Evil Eye*

— eye of Horus, eye of Ra, eye of Bast-Sekhmet, Uraeus-Wadjet, protect your child here from harm, from ill intent — thanked the magus profusely, who never broke the strange little smile on her face and simply said, "On your way" and I quickly passed on to the Musaion, seriously spooked, before I realized my conundrum.

Obviously, I could not show my philosopher colleagues that I had a charm, they would laugh it off as native superstition — any hint of a peculiarity or mannerism that was non-Greek instantly noted by them, cataloged, to be met with severe contempt or cajoling in the gymnasium at the next available opportunity. I was already treated like a prize pig on account of my complexion and hair. I did not need to give any more openings.

On the other hand, this missive had come from the world of the Gods, which was, well, serious. I was in trouble, perhaps damned by Hyginos whether I wore the wadjet or not. I was not entirely sure what was going on, but I knew at this point that what I had thought was another of Sumethres' pranks was clearly part of a larger drama, equally divine as well as human. Despite all my other mannerisms, Greek habits and dress, peripateticism, my service to the King as a philosopher — the Goddess was right, I was Egyptian. I could not think to ignore her.

But I did not know what I should do. I settled on stowing the charm in the folds of the toga, hoisting it like I was climbing the stairs, and entering the Musaion from the front. It would be best not to be seen sneaking around.

If I had hoped to pass to my cell unnoticed, this was foiled almost the moment I stepped between the braziers in the portico. There were three men standing in the ante-chamber before the peripatos in animated discussion, who called out when I approached. Rats.

"Psamethes," said one, Orestes, who could never pronounce my name, "Psamethes, we are in crisis."

"What is this crisis?" I said in Greek, smiling my face into a mask.

"Calliodoros says that you have taken three copies of the *Pinakes*. We need them back now, because there is a dispute involving cataloging." This came from Zeno, a quiet, sallow man with lazy eyes who never seemed to look direct-ly at me.

"What?" I said, "Why would I take three copies of *Pinakes*? What on Earth would I do with them?"

"But we are aware," said the third, Philo, "That you are one who Hermes smiles upon; that you have been among the books."

Weird. "I'm sorry, what does that have to do with anything?" I said, "This is the Musaion, it is for the books?"

"Or the books are for it," said Orestes, pointedly. "Or for the King, and the Gods."

"I do not have any scrolls of *Pinakes*, and I have no use for it. I am studying mechanics and physics for these past six months, and only at the blessing of the King, need I

13

remind you, am I even here. So tell me what is the meaning of this, who has claimed that I, of all people, would get involved in a dispute involving the Library Catalog?"

"Calliodoros heard it from Sophistic Solon." General sniggers through the group, *what?* "Who has it on the authority of one Hyginos that you took three volumes from Apollodorus because you were not aware of the alphabet and needed to brush up on your letters." Howls of laughter.

"Perhaps," said Philo, "If we wrote aleph in the shape of an ox it would be more transparent for you?"

"Hilarious," I said. "Very funny. Yet is it still the consensus of you gentlemen that I am digging through the work of Callimachus to upset the order of the library and spread general chaos?"

"In all seriousness," said Orestes, wiping tears from his eyes. "Apollodorus has misplaced three volumes, cannot find them anywhere, and a delegation from Cyrene is about to arrive. Your name came up from Hyginos and we thought to investigate before going to Eratosthenes. Someone will get whipped for this for sure."

"Ah," I said. "So you needed someone to take the fall."

"Well, on account of your literacy," said Philo, falling into snorts of laughter again.

"It's really not that funny," I said. "It doesn't even make sense."

"The truth is no one's blaming you Psa," said Zeno.

"We just haven't been able to find you all day. Where have you been?"

"Out. Busy. Errands," I said evasively. Then, seeing them all standing there expectantly: "I was visiting family." All Egyptians are family.

"Oh," said Orestes, raising his eyebrows. "I did not know you had any family living in Alexandria. I thought you came from Sais."

"Oh, some people have relocated recently," I said evasively. "You know, the nilometer has been low the past few years." General grunts and nods of assent. "Distant relatives on my father's side, a foreign city, good to help them settle in."

"A good man looks to his society, a great man looks after his blood," said Orestes. "Just to be sure, you really don't have the volumes of *Pinakes*, right?"

"Right," I said. "And, uh, why was it that Hyginos thought I had these scrolls again?"

15

\wedge\wedge\wedge\wedge\wedge\wedge

The first thing I did when I got back to my cell was search it. I knew the Greeks, and I had been through this kind of thing before. There was a high likelihood someone had planted the *Pinakes* in my cot so that they could be "discovered" later, and I would be subject to a flogging. But I found nothing. All my items were in their normal place: the ostracon with the prayers to Osiris written on them, my oil lamps and incense cubes (well hidden), even the letter from my Father in demotic, my most valued possession. It was clear no one had been there. Still, my heart was not calm.

Hyginos' name had popped up three times in the past three hours, once from the lips of a God. I searched my mind to see if I could remember anything that I had done that might have brought on his ire — during my first half-year at the Musaion I had done my best to stay out of everyone's way.

Hyginos, much more than Sophistic Solon — who I was pretty sure at this point was a joke, a fictional character who did not exist, although I was not positive — he was an orator. He was passionate, sensuous, outspoken, and had gained a reputation throughout the city for Greek supremacy. To an extreme degree. The one thing I could get my Jewish debating buddies to agree on was that we all hated Hyginos, which was rare; Jews almost always preferred a Greek to an Egyptian, but Hyginos had one day gone into the agora with a small gong and shouted a series of proclamations relating how Yahweh was in fact an incarnation of Helios, making few friends for himself but eliciting a great deal of cow dung before fleeing a commotion which almost became a riot.

He was a peripatetic, so he claimed. Or was he? I was not really sure where Hyginos stood philosophically. He seemed to maintain a wide social circle, while having few real friends. But he could stir up a firestorm. Always one for flamboyant gestures, he would turn the smallest slight into the greatest controversy, somehow managing to avoid blame. Had I spoken with him? I leafed through the papyrus scrolls of my days, stored on the featureless racks of memory, each day seeming the same as any other. He had mocked me once as a degenerate barbarian; I had quoted Sonchis of Sais to him, what he had said to the *real* Solon, "All Greeks are Children." I thought it might lead to a fight, was scared of it, but he liked that — he had laughed and clapped me on the shoulder, said I was the first Egyptian he could respect. I had no idea how sincere he was at the time. Was that all? That was months ago.

Of course all my Egyptian friends hated him. He deliberately committed sacrilege whenever he could. He wanted the maximum amount of attention possible. But it did not seem like I had ever done anything to earn Hyginos' disdain, on the contrary, he had been almost...amiable. A fact I had tried to keep from everyone. Of course, he was not a particularly predictable person.

At this moment there was a call from the hall outside my door, starting me out of my thoughts. A herald. I gathered up the folds of my toga — oops, the wadjet was still in there, got to pick that up too, hide that — and walked to the door. A young herald was standing in the doorframe, in a chiton the color of Tyre. "Hail, Psammethicus! The Librarian, Erathosthenes, wishes to see you."

All the curses in all the languages I knew went through my heart, failed, and fell out of my heart again. "Wonderful," I said. "Please, give me a moment to collect my belongings." I went back inside. What belongings? Those - those - bastards! Had they really ratted me out to the Head Librarian on account of my race? Low, low, low, even for them. I could already feel the lashes on my back, I was cringing, my heart was a bird that wanted to escape its chest. There was no proof, but would it matter?

"Follow me," said the herald when I came back out from my chambers. I had done nothing but put the wadjet openly on my chest. If I was to be beaten for the sole crime of Being Egyptian In The Library Of Alexandria, I might as well do it with pride. And perhaps the Gods would protect me.

Thoth gives Maat to the doer of Maat, to the speaker of Maat, I silently prayed, hardly realizing I had slipped back into my old language, as I followed the scribe through the arches of the peripatos. There were people staring, but, well, they always stared. I caught sight of Zeno, decidedly not looking at me, as usual — was that an apologetic look on his face? I didn't have time to reflect on this before we passed through the temenos and into the house of the scrolls.

To my surprise Eratosthenes was waiting for us just beyond the double doors, hands clasped in front of him. "Ah, Psammetichus, our newest scholar. I appreciate your coming so promptly."

"Librarian Eratosthenes," I said in flawless Greek, inclining my head.

"Please," he said, "The title is unnecessary. You may leave us, Chiron." The herald bowed and departed.

"Psa," said Eratosthenes, "Sunset is nearly upon us. Would you accompany an old man to the roof Observatory? I wish to witness the rising of Aphrodite."

Okay. So. Not getting beaten. Today. "Certainly, sir,"

I said.

We started the walk down the line of the stacks, the papyrus scrolls catching the evening light from the open temenos. "I notice," said Eratosthenes, "That you wear a traditional charm of your people tonight."

Great. "Oh this?" I said, "This is nothing, lord, just a bauble."

"A bauble eh?" said Eratosthenes, smirking. "I have heard that the eye of Horus, whom we call Apollo, protects from the Evil Eye. Is this true?"

"There are some among my people who would claim, sir."

"And your people are great magicians are they not?"

Here we go. "So they say, sir."

Eratosthenes laughed, a big booming laugh that surprised me, filling up the whole of the stacks. The remaining scribes shelving looked at us, shocked. "Well said. I have often thought that what your people do might not, strictly speaking, be called *magic* — if you speak the language of the Gods that is. The Babylonians seem to have more exorcists." He smiled again.

I was unsure if he was baiting me. You could never tell with the Greeks. "Sir," I said, "With respect, our civilization is older than the Babylonians, thousands of years older, sir."

"Ah yes," said Eratosthenes, "I never denied that. I am familiar with what old Manetho, on whose acclaimed recommendation you have come here to us, has written. I was merely commenting on matters of *theology*."

"Right." I said. What did that mean? He was incomprehensible. Then again, this was the man who had proved, *mathematically proved,* that the Earth is round.

"Ah, here we are," said the Head Librarian. We had reached the side staircase which led to the roof terrace. "Help an old man up would you?"

I gave Eratosthenes my arm, trying not to think about how peculiar this was. Had any other novice scholar been treated in this way? I had never heard about Orestes or Zeno being the Librarian's personal escort. What was the catch — was he going to throw me off the roof, instead of beating me? I shuddered.

"You know," said Eratosthenes, as if catching my thought, "There are some who forget, very quickly, that our philosophy and religion originally came from the Egyptians."

I opened my mouth and closed it again; I could think of nothing to say.

"But the memories of men are short. No sooner has the sword conquered the plow than memory gives way to forgetfulness. That's what libraries are for." He smiled at me.

"You think, sir?" I said.

"Of course — why else has our King elected to call our renowned institution the House of the Muses?"

"I don't understand."

"Ah," he sighed, "I forget, you are not Greek. Mnemnosyne - memory! She is the Mother of the Muses, surely you must know that?"

Kicking myself. "Of course sir, I had known that," and it was true, I had, "I just forgot."

We were reaching the top of the staircase now. "You are nervous. Why?"

I decided frank honesty was the best bet. "I was wondering why you had called me, sir."

He laughed again, now a deep throated chuckle. "You think I am going to punish you for some imaginary transgression."

"I had wondered."

"No, no, I was telling the truth, I need to witness the rising of Aphrodite and thought a young man such as yourself could give me a hand here." We sat on the parapet. The Royal Quarter spread out before us. The Palace of the King was glinting in the setting Sun, beyond you could see the Jewish ghetto, and then, even more impoverished, the Egyptian slum. A sea-wind came from the North, off the harbor.

"Right on time," said Eratosthenes. "Now, before the planet, or the Goddess, rises, let us have a brief discussion. Tell me your philosophical views, Psa."

I was flummoxed. This was the last thing I had expected. A test?

"Well, sir," I said, searching for the words. "Like most

men of my race, I hold that the first element to exist was Water."

Eratosthenes nodded.

"Subsequently, there was Earth, arising from the Water in a heap. Then, Earth and Air separated into the Empyrean and the Kosmos."

Eratosthenes said, "So I have heard, and so your countryman Manetho reports in his book on your Physics."

"Then you know that the emergence of Fire occurred when the Cosmic Egg was split, and from this was born Helios, the Sun."

"Hmm, these are well known," said Eratosthenes. "But what are your *philosophical* views?"

"Come again?" I said. "Those are my philosophical views."

"Yes, yes, I understand that these are your views on the cosmogony, in keeping with all your people. But what of our philosophy? Do you follow Plato, or his pupil?"

What was he playing at? "Well, Plato of course. He is the one who is closest to the teachings of my countrymen; many of his teachings are our teachings. In fact, they even came from my home city, the city of my family. I mean, I think Aristotle is in harmony with Plato." Erathosthenes shifted slightly. *what was going on.* "But to me Plato is the primary of the two." I thought it was a good answer, educated, well-rounded, true both to me and to my culture.

"Ah! Good," said Eratosthenes. "That is what I

thought."

He got up and started pacing. The Sun was setting. If he wanted to view the rising of Aphrodite now would be a good time to look for it. Then he stared right at me.

"You see, Psa," he said, "You have not picked a side."

My heart. "A side?" The same as the Goddess. This day.

"Yes, a side." Eratosthenes clasped his hands again. "Most scholars at this point have reached a decisive stance whether they are for Idealism or Formalism, and it is this rift which currently splits this Academy — perhaps inferior to the Academy of Plato, but a dwelling for the Muses all the same. You had not heard?"

"Well, no," I said, "I had heard whispers. But I did not think it really concerned me."

"Extraordinary," said Eratosthenes. "Hyginos has been attempting to recruit you to the Formalists for the past three months, and you have not even noticed."

"What?" I said.

"I will chalk it up to the fact that you are not of the same race as the rest of us. Indeed, you are the first Egyptian to matriculate in the Musaion."

Of that I was well aware.

"So you are telling me," I said slowly, "That there is a dispute in the Musaion of Alexandria."

"Correct," said Eratosthenes.

"Between followers of Plato and followers of Aristotle?"

"Roughly," he said. "But it's a bit more complicated."

"How so?"

"Well Psa," and he sat back down next to me. "I have a problem. I do not know where all the books that are in the Library of Alexandria are."

What? "But you are the Head Librarian."

"Correct," said Eratosthenes.

"So..." I said, "Isn't that your job?"

"Quite right!" said Eratosthenes. "Absolutely correct. In fact, the King would have my head if he learned the truth. The Library is the kingdom's greatest asset, which differentiates it from the other parts of Alexander's Empire - aside from the warlord's tomb, of course."

Did he just call Alexander the Great "the warlord"?

"Now, you think that this debate that we are having — between the Idealists and the Formalists — does not concern you. But in fact it does. You already have a side, although you do not know it. You unthinkingly take the side of Plato; like me, you are an Idealist."

Understanding dawned. "You want me to join your team."

"No, that is not what I said at all. I said you already are on a side without knowing it. Luckily for both of us, you have not actually chosen either side consciously yet."

"I'm confused."

"I'm not surprised. Allow me to explain. I do not

know where all the books are in the Library of Alexandria because the Formalists have been hiding them from me. Not only that, they are plotting to gain control of the Library Catalog. There are now five different copies of the late Callimachus' *Pinakes* circulating, none of them complete. No one knows which is the original and which is the forgery so who can say which books actually are or are not in the Library, or where they are located, and it is too much for any one man to know."

"So you're a figurehead," I said.

"Don't be ridiculous, my son!" It was almost like I had offended him. "There are still many sections of the Library that I do control. The point is that for years now, under my nose, a second library has been constructed. The Library of the Ulterior."

"A second library?" The Sun was setting. With a flash I realized that if I was to meet Sumenthres — by the Gods that seemed a long time ago — I needed to leave now.

"Yes. And I want you to infiltrate it."

"Come again?"

"You are Egyptian, this makes you a natural Idealist. No one is sure which side you are on. I want you to approach Hyginos - no doubt you have worked out now that he is the loudest of the Formalists, though he is not their leader - and become his friend."

Great, I thought. *And I'm supposed to break into his house tonight.*

"Sir," I said. "What if what I said was true? I really do not think it concerns me."

"By the Judgement of Paris!" said Eratosthenes. "Men like you, in the agora, who always sit on the fence, I despise more than any other. I have told you that you already have a side without knowing it; luckily no one here has been able to work out which side you are actually on. Think about it. And when you have made your decision you can find a way to send word to me in secret. And who knows — if you really are perplexed and can't make a decision, you can always ask Sophistic Solon."

I was winded by the time I made it to the home of Unathes. He lived in the nicest part of the Egyptian slum, which meant he had a manor with a miniature shrine to Osiris out front. A circle of people, about twelve, were waiting for me in an alcove between his stoop and the shrine.

"Psst, Psa, you idiot," Sumethres whispered, "Why did you come dressed as an Egyptian?"

"I didn't want anyone to know —"

"That you are a member of that Academy? We had counted on you coming as a Greek. You are always wearing a toga and flaunting your Greek mannerisms — now in the one moment when the rest of us need to appear as Greek you come here looking like an Egyptian!" Low sniggers were spreading across the group.

"Classic," said Unathes. "Okay, does anyone have an extra toga?"

"I'm sorry," I said, "I've had a really busy day."

"Yes, yes, we know how much more important you are than the rest of us since you are a Greek scholar. Why can't you just think and let the Gods inspire you rather than philosophically yammering on —"

"Mirini," said Unathes to his wife, who had just come outside, "Do we have an extra toga?"

"Are you going to tell me what you're doing?" she shot back.

"Oho!" someone said. "The protectress of the house speaks!"

"It's men's business," Unathes said. "Just trust me."

"Husband, I do trust you," Mirini said, "Only it looks like you are about to do sorcery."

"No, we're not," said Unathes. "That's just what it looks like. Sumethres, what's the plan again?"

"Now that our dear friend Psammethicus," he cuffed me on the head, "has graced us with his presence I can lay out the plan." He paused, a bit too long, and we waited anxiously. "Which is, gentlemen, sorcery."

A couple of groans went through the group. I felt my heart sink into my toes. Just what I needed now. Black magic.

"We are going to put a curse on Hyginos cows."

"Hyginos has cows?" said a youth, Irihor, by the sound of him.

"Yes," said Sumethres, "Three of them."

"And Sumethres," said Mirini, "How are you going to

put the curse on these cows?"

He grew uncomfortable. He started fidgeting, not meeting her eyes. "Well. I thought we would leave a small statue of Typhon and...use the Evil Eye."

"The Evil Eye?" said Mirini.

"Yes," said Sumethres. "Everyone knows it works on cattle. Why, in my old village there was an old man who once lost three calves —"

"This is what I am talking about," said Mirini to her husband. "None of you men actually know a thing about magic."

"I'm sorry?" said Unathes.

"All I'm saying is you should probably talk to a woman first. If you want to put a curse on this man's property, leaving an icon is going to do next to nothing for the spell but it will alert the whole town that the people who messed with this man's cows were Egyptians and not Greeks regardless of the costumes you wear."

There was general silence at this. She was making sense.

"So, what, then, sorceress, should we do?" Unathes said to his wife.

"Obviously you need to make a living sacrifice. Hold on, I'll get you a chicken." She vanished into the house and laughter began to spread across the group again.

"Unathes," someone said, "You have quite a wife."

"I know, I am a lucky man," he said. "Now what was

the rest of the plan, Sumethres, for the costumes?"

"I have," said Sumethres, hauling a massive linen bag out of nowhere, "managed to pilfer these."

"Which are?" said Unathes.

"Masks," said Sumethres, "From one of the Greek ritual pageants."

We were going to curse Hyginos' cattle disguised as a Greek chorus.

"Perfect," said Unathes. "Where do you get this stuff?"

"Oh, I'm a man about town," said Sumethres. "I'm in business across all these corridors —"

"Okay. Forget I asked," said Unathes. "It's a great idea, Sumet."

We passed the masks around, quickly donning them. I got a distorted face in the throes of sorrow. Tragedy.

Mirini returned with a chicken struggling in a bag. "I've clamped its beak shut. And I've got his toga here — my sister does laundry for that Greek woman, the wife of the harbormaster. You just have to bring it back unsoiled, you understand?" She tossed it to me.

"Thank you," said Unathes.

"Now you listen to me," she said. We gathered around, huddling under her from where she stood on the stoop. "Cut the chicken's head with a single blow. Paint the lintel and the door frame with the chicken's blood and leave the body *lying in the threshold.* Then say this incantation over his cattle." She said some words which I will not repeat here. "I've just taught you woman's magic - and do not forget it!"

We, the conspirators, donned the rest of our gear, and were off with hardly another word.

Things were going smoothly until Osarseph, my nemesis, showed up. Drunk, as usual.

"Players!" he called out. "Where are you going so fast?"

"The body of Osiris," Sumethres swore, or prayed.

We had passed down the causeway near the edge of the Jewish Quarter. This was the darkest part of town, and the easiest place to go undetected. It ran next to the canal, and none of the guards patrolled here. Unfortunately it also took us right next to the ale-houses which some of my favorite debating buddies frequented.

He was right next to me, somehow. "I recognize the cut of that toga!" He burped. "It has the royal insignia on it. Has our harbormaster taken to playing Dionysus?"

The others were looking at me, nervous - about half had raced off, quickly into the night, on towards the Greek quarter, not needing to be captured.

"Psa —" Sumethres hissed. "Just run!" I saw Unathes standing a few paces off, half in and half out of the light — wise enough not to let a single member of the group get caught.

"What's the matter?" said Osarseph. "Cat got your tongue?"

For some reason I never understood afterwards, this got to me. Perhaps it had been the day, what with the schemes, the oracle, the bullying, and the growing sense that I was a mouse caught in a trap and the granary was soon to be flooded - but suddenly what flashed before my eyes was the image of Hyginos, lighting the cat sacred to Bast on fire, and laughing as it burned. And as every Egyptian knows, the other side of Bast is Sekhmet, and I felt her rear up in me.

"Like you would know, Jew!" I spat.

"Great," Sumethres said, turning towards the canal. "Now he decides to be patriotic. Just great."

"I know that voice!" said Osarseph. "This is the voice of Psammetichus!" Luckily no one else was there, but was he *drunk*. He knocked the mask from my face. "Why are you disguising yourself as the harbormaster? What Egyptian trickery is this?"

"Psa," said Unathes. "Not the time for a battle."

"No less than Jewish trickery!" I shouted.

"What? Are you going to enslave me again?"

"There was never any enslavement — Moses. Was.

Egyptian."

"*Psa,*" Unathes hissed. "Now is *not the time.*"

Osarseph burped. "And the Queen of Sheba was Greek."

"In fact," I said — Sumethres was tugging on my robes — "This Amenophis son of Hapu, who advised King Amenophis in the time of my forefathers - he said that Moses was none other than King of the Lepers!"

"Come on Psa, this is not an ale-hall, it doesn't matter," said Sumethres, trying to lead me away.

"Wait," said Osarseph, gradually coming to consciousness of something. "There are more of you. What are you doing tonight?"

"That's enough," said Unathes commandingly.

I said: "We are going to Hyginos' house to avenge ourselves."

Both of the older men gasped. "Psa, you complete idiot! You, you, *nark.*" Sumethres was almost lost for words.

I held up a hand. "Wait," I said, smiling. "I know this asshole."

"Hyginos?" said Osarseph. "You are going to Hyginos?"

"Yes," I said.

"That's the one Greek I hate more than you Egyptians."

"Yes, I know."

"Well how can I join you?"

"Psa, this is a *bad idea*."

"Wait," said Unathes. "It might be the only idea left. Do you have any extra masks?"

"Who is this," said Irihor, "And why is he coming with us?"

"Because Psammethicus is a Greek Egyptian who wishes he were a Jew," they replied.

"Ah. Of course," said Irihor. We were about a block from Hyginos' manor, crouching in the shadows of a Temple of Hecate. Travelers and magicians sheltered here from the Sun. Stranger things than a chorus of Greek Egyptians materializing out of the night had happened on her doorstep.

"What's the plan?" said Osarseph.

"You and Psammethicus keep watch," said Sumethres. "We need a team to go to the paddock where the cows are kept, and we need at least one pair of eyes on every lane. The others should be coming back soon, we can get into position then if the ground is safe. I want you two to coordinate between the paddock and the door. Unathes and I will do the deed."

"What deed?" said Osarseph.

"I'll tell you later," I said.

He mumbled something like, "Egyptian trickery."

"Hush!" said Sumethres. "Here they come."

Ptahmedjes and Ita emerged from the shadows. "It is clear," said Ptah. "The house is silent; there is not even a lamp lit within. If we are quick, and quiet..."

"Alright," said Sumethres, "Everyone has their positions, let's move, and Psa —" He gestured to me.

"Yes?"

"If anything happens with the drunk, if you come out alive, I'll make you wish you were never born."

"Sumet," Unathes chided. "It's fine."

"I've been planning this for weeks, he's not going to cock it up now."

"Alright," I said. "Alright."

I heard when Unathes and Sumet cut off the head of the chicken. It made a dull thump that resounded through the alley. Osarseph and I were just around the corner, crouching in the door frame of a house that was abandoned, or never completed, it was hard to tell. Around the other corner was the paddock at the back of the house. Ptahmejes, Ita and Irihor were there, to put a spell on the cows.

"What was that?" said Osarseph.

"The head of a chicken," I whispered back.

"What? Is that a code?"

"No, numbskull," I said. "The literal head of a chicken."

"Why are you beheading a chicken?"

"They're going to paint the door frame with it."

"Sacrilege!"

"What?"

"This is what the Lord commanded the Israelites to do on the first Passover. Why do you disgusting creatures always pervert all that is holy?"

"Come again?"

"With your animal-headed gods and perverse rituals, you dirty lughead."

"And now *you* are perverting all that I find holy."

"No, you do not understand — the angel of the Lord came to take all the firstborn, and only by painting the door-frame in this way could the tithe be avoided. Pharaoh's children were all killed."

"Where do you get this stuff?"

"Here — again, you are trying to rewrite history."

"Well it's not in any of our records."

"That's because, you heathens, you are constantly pretending you are animals and fornicating and inventing false History."

"Can you just be quiet? You're forgetting we have a common enemy here."

"Now you are going to say that the pyramids were not built by slaves."

"That's it!" I whispered furiously. "I've had enough! The pyramids were not built by slaves, it was paid labour. There are *records*. I have *read* them. And the pyramids were built before your people even *existed* or at least when you were all desert nomads in the Yemen."

Osarseph looked at me for a second with a lazy eye. Even with the mask on I could tell he was more drunk than I had thought. Then, calculated, he said: "They were granaries."

I went to punch him. He ducked. He scurried away and then tripped over his sandals and fell in the dust.

Realizing my mistake — he was in danger of blowing the whole operation — I jumped after him and tried to grab his toga, but he thought I was still out for him and pulled away around the corner. "Osarseph," I hissed as loudly as I dared. "Come back and be quiet."

I went around the corner. Already he was not there. Shit. I was about to go on when suddenly, with a start, I noticed there was someone watching me from inside the house.

The window was perfectly round, and it had a round shutter. In the center of the shutter was a brass knob, and it was flung wide open in a niche, or alcove, between two corners. The inside of the house was lit by a single oil lamp, and must have contained mirrors, because it seemed to go on an impossibly long distance. But strangest was the fact that standing at the window was the face and body of a troglodyte.

A troglodyte? It was unmistakable. Grey skin was hanging in folds from his arms, white hair flowing from a spotted scalp, and tufts of whiskers poking from his ears and above his lips. It was a troglodyte, a cave dweller —

what was a troglodyte doing in a house? What was a troglodyte doing in *Hyginos'* house?

He turned, expressionless and without a sound, and walked down the impossibly long corridor I saw extending behind the window. Was that it? Had I just blown our cover? Would he wake them up — wait, could troglodytes even talk? What was one of them doing inside?

The oil lamp went out, and I could no longer see the magically infinite corridor. Suddenly remembering myself, I plunged around the corner and ran right into Ptahmedjes, Ita and Irihor, carrying Osarseph between them.

"Psa," said Ptahmedjes, "This was supposed to be your responsibility."

"Yes, I know, sorry," I said.

"He said you got into a brawl," said Ita.

"You Egyptians," Osarseph slurred, "Always betray me."

"You nearly betrayed *us* you goon," I whispered.

"Don't bother," said Irihor. "We're done. We're meeting back at the temple."

I followed behind them, feeling conflicted, but also pondering the mystery of the troglodyte in the window.

ℓ

Sumethres was very happy with how it had all turned out, so happy he had forgotten Osarseph was even there, and the next time I ran into either of them it was together; they were out drinking together. The madness of the caper, not to mention its success, had made friends of us all. We were all elated for several days — that is, until the consequences of our actions began to spread around the city.

When I got back to my cell that night I was exhausted from the events of the day. There was too much to take in, and I could not begin to make sense of it all. I threw myself onto my cot and passed out almost at once. Unfortunately, this did not bring me peace.

In my dreams I wandered to the West, my soul nearing the Atlas mountains and the City of the Dead. I saw it, rising from the desert of Libya, a step pyramid silhouetted against rays of blinding light, and grey figures surrounding it - were they troglodytes? My sleep became troubled. Words in languages I did not understand passed through my thoughts.

Then I woke with a start. There was something standing at the foot of my bed.

I peeked over my linen bedclothes and stared at the specter. It was glowing a soft white light.

I was trembling. My tongue stuck to the roof of my mouth.

The ghost made the gesture whereby a child says it wants to eat, or a grown man indicates he has something important to say. Thumb pointing inward.

"Who — who are you?" I said.

The ghost breathed its name over me, and I felt the breath of centuries pass over my head as it dissolved: *"Im-houthes."*

I awoke to someone pounding at my door.

"Psa! Psammetichus!"

I was up. The Sun was out. What time was it?

"Yes?" I called.

"Psammetichus, the delegation from Cyrene has ar-rived. You are required in the forecourt. All the scholars are, and you are not present. Come quickly!"

I pulled myself out of bed, quickly washing my face, and was out in the corridor in about half a minute. I was still wearing the harbourmaster's toga — acceptable? Probably, it was fringed. Looked formal. Passable.

"Did you oversleep?" said the herald when I came out the door. "Long night?"

"You could say that," I said.

"An excess of drinking does not become a scholar, you know."

I ignored this. "There is a delegation from Cyrene?"

"You had not heard? Some very, very important people have arrived, and every scholar sponsored by the King is required to welcome them."

"When?"

"Well, now, sir." But I was already running as fast as I could towards the forecourt.

I flew through the peripatos and came right to the same alcove where I had encountered Orestes, Zeno and Philo yesterday, and yes, practically the whole Academy was there. I quickly hastened to a place at the back of the crowd, there, I was next to Zeno.

"Hm," he said, as usual without looking at me, "What kept you?"

"I overslept."

"Right. Were you visiting other relatives?"

I never had the chance to reply because at that moment someone blew a horn.

"The delegation from Cyrene greets the honorable Eratosthenes, and attendant Musaion: in the name of Zeus, in the name of Serapis!"

Then I could see Eratosthenes was in front of the crowd, and he stepped forward, to greet the herald, and the crowd of men with their pages. They were not all old, some were rather young, or at least middle-aged. Many were wearing the distinctive toga in the purple of Tyre. These men had wealth.

"It is my honor to greet men such as this from my

home country," Eratosthenes responded, very formally, more formally than I had ever heard him speak — which was not often, I supposed.

It was then I noticed a man who stood apart from the rest. He looked - well, I do not know how to say what he looked like, except that I had never seen an uglier person in my entire life. He was so catastrophically ugly it was fascinating, he seemed almost divine. When I first saw him my mind instantly went to the image of the god Hephaistos, working in his forge in the fire-mountains of Syracuse. His eyes were too wide, spaced far out on his skull, and his nose was too large, and asymmetrical. He was not short, but he seemed hunched, as if he was carrying a great weight. He was not actually deformed, but somehow he seemed it — in fact, I myself felt upon looking at him as though *I* were deformed. It was a curious sensation. But when I looked into his eyes I got a sense of his spirit, and then I saw what Mind he had.

Everyone else was treating him with an extreme amount of deference.

"It is a great honor," Eratosthenes was saying, "To have you here attending in our library."

"Oh, of course," the man was saying. "I studied here myself once. And it is the most important library in the world."

"Who is that?" I whispered.

"Archimedes of Syracuse," several voices hissed.

Archimedes walked with Eratosthenes up the stairs, as the delegation began to enter the forecourt. Our crowd parted. Apparently that was the whole of the ceremony, for now.

"It has not changed much," I heard him saying. "Even the smell is the same."

"We have made some new improvements," said Eratosthenes. "We have new volumes from the East which may be of interest to you. Mechanics."

"Oh?" said Archimedes. "Wonderful. I look forward to them." They passed down the hall, with the rest of the Cyrenians and their heralds and their pages, leaving us, junior scholars, in our alcove.

"Who is that?" said Orestes laughing. "Honestly, why even let an Egyptian enter the Musaion?"

"Hm," said Zeno, gazing abstractedly toward the horizon. "For that matter, why would we let in most Greeks?"

Orestes chose to ignore this. "So. Psammetichus. Do you have any plans today?"

Plans. "Well," I said slowly. "I think I am going to look through some of the Babylonian scrolls. I am trying to compare Berossos and Manetho. Obviously, I seek to prove the antiquity of my own civilization."

Orestes wrinkled his nose. "Ugh. Why go to those copy-cats for History? Why not just read Herodotus?"

"You know," said Philo, "I think Hyginos could help

you with that. He would probably be best for finding those volumes. But where is he? I don't think I saw him at the ceremony."

"That's right," said Zeno. "He wasn't there. It's unlike him."

At that moment we saw Hyginos, moving very quickly down the street, and hurrying up the stairs before the portico.

"You're late," said Orestes.

"Confound it all!" shouted Hyginos. "It's your fault!" he said, pointing at me.

"Me?" I said. For a wild moment I thought the troglodyte had actually mentioned —

"Well, not your fault, but clearly the fault of your countrymen. Brothers, I have been the victim of a strange conspiracy. A curse, clearly, of the worst variety — but I have yet to discover the cause."

"A curse?" said Philo. "Isn't that a bit fanciful?"

"You will not think so when you hear what I have to say."

We waited. Hyginos was out of breath. He was carrying a bundle of scrolls under one arm.

"This morning," he said, "I left my house to attend the ceremony. But before I could leave I discovered the door-frame had been painted with blood. Not only that, before it was the body of a headless chicken. Now, brothers, tell me what is the meaning of this? Clearly it cannot be anything less than Egyptian devilry, concocted against me on account of the fact I am so unpopular with the natives."

"Well I must say, Hyginos," was Zeno still just staring off into space? "I must say that you have not been the most skilled at making friends."

"But we are in luck," said Hyginos, "For we have an Egyptian here. Tell me my friend, what is the meaning of this act of your countrymen? What ill will do they have towards me? And will this magic lead either me or my family to a bad end?"

I thought for a moment. "I do not think I have ever heard of an Egyptian doing something like that. It is not our way to use an animal in such fashion. However, I have heard from the Jewish scriptures that the same was done by the Israelites to keep the archon of their God from taking the firstborn child of their families at the first Passover. In which case, Hyginos: perhaps it is a blessing."

I went into the great hall of the scrolls to search for a book. When I got there I found the same herald waiting for me.

"What, you again?" I said.

He did not laugh. "Eratosthenes asks for you."

Great. He probably wanted me to tell him whether I would go along with his plan. And I had been too busy to even think about what he had said, let alone consider it in all its implications. "Very well," I said. "Lead the way."

The herald led me down a passage I had never been to before, and up a stairwell to the second story. He stopped by a pair of oak double doors and bowed. "They are in here," he said. Then he turned and left, and I watched him vanish into the distance. He had never done that before, the bowing.

I knocked on the doors. "Enter!" a voice called from inside. I opened them and stepped into a warm hall with low tables. There was a fireplace, and a fire was lit. Wine had been poured in many bronze bowls, I could smell it. Standing at the far end were Archimedes and Eratosthenes, and a couple of attendant pages.

"Ah, Psammetichus, wonderful," said Eratosthenes. "I was mentioning to my colleague here that we had a new Egyptian student, moreover one who was interested in mechanics, and he wanted to meet you."

I stepped forward, suddenly intimidated, unsure how deferential I was meant to be.

Archimedes did not smile when he looked at me, but I could tell from his eyes that he was interested. 'Greetings, sir," I said. "It is an honor to meet you."

"Poo on honor," said Archimedes. "I would rather you tell me how to find the area under an irregular curve."

"I do not understand," I said. "It is a curve. It does not have area."

"According to whom?"

"According to Euclid," I said.

"I know more about Euclid than you will forget in ten lifetimes," he said. "But they say that your people invented geometry."

"This is true," I said proudly.

"Then you must have secrets that you have not told."

"If this is true, I have not been initiated into them."

"And that is exactly the same thing you would say if you had," said Archimedes.

"Yes. Precisely," I said.

"Glad to see you two are getting along," said Eratosthenes. "Care for any refreshments?"

"I am not hungry," said Archimedes. "We ate this morning at the inn."

"Psa?" said Eratosthenes.

I was famished. "I would not mind some bread."

"Very well," said Eratosthenes, who gestured to the pages. "Psa comes to us with an Egyptian orientation towards physics, but he has been very interested in mechanics. He was recommended by the priest Manetho himself."

"What is your interest in mechanics?" asked Archimedes.

"I want to invent a new kind of shaduf," I said.

"What is a shaduf?"

"It is a sort of lever, which draws water from an irrigation ditch," I said, trying to illustrate with my hands, but he waved an arm.

"Yes, I know what you are talking about. I have seen these things. Do you know anything about sphere-making?" said Archimedes.

"I do not understand what you mean. I am no sculptor."

"No, boy, sphere-making. I am talking about machines which reflect the heavens."

The existence of such things had not occurred to me. "How?"

"Driven by gears. I will show you. I have written a book. The scribes are copying it as we speak for it to be put into the library."

"So then, sir, the spheres would model the motion of the planets, and allow us to see their curves?"

"Precisely," said Archimedes. "I can see you are, in fact, a geometer. Do you know Eudoxus?"

"Yes, sir, I have heard of him."

"Then you will know he studied at Heliopolis."

"So even my own priests have told me."

"I have questions for the priests of that city."

"Of what sort, sir?"

"I would like to know what they taught to Pythagoras."

"That is forbidden, sir," I said.

"So even the Pythagoreans themselves say. But is it true," Archimedes reclined onto one of the benches by the low tables, "Is it true what they, such as Philolaus, say - that in fact the Earth revolves around a central fire?"

"I am not a priest of our Helios, sir," I said.

"See," said Archimedes to the Head Librarian, "He knows something. You can tell."

"You know that Aristarchus of Samos has just written a book on this?" said Eratosthenes. "If you are so interested in the topic I can have it brought to you."

"Can you also have brought the works of Antiphon the Sophist on his method of exhaustion? This is the key, old friend, the key to integrating under an irregular curve."

"So you say. So you have told me for years now - I swear you said the same thing to me thirty years ago."

"Nonsense, I just had this revelation last week," said Archimedes.

"Does not Eudoxus develop Antiphon's method, sirs?" I said.

"See, the lad has good memory. I could use him," said Archimedes. Eratosthenes only shook his head. "This is true, you are quite correct, although I do not think you know quite what it is you are saying. You see, it is like this. Take a cone. Slice it into parts. Slice it one way you get a sphere, another an ellipse, still another a parabola. However, slice it in a perpendicular fashion and you find a hyperbola."

"A what?" I said.

"See, this is a kind of geometry your people did *not* invent," said Archimedes airily. "But I tell you, I can find the area of a sphere, or an ellipse, even a parabola. But I cannot find the area underneath that final curve, and I *will* know it." He pounded a fist on the table. "How many grains of sand would it take to fill up the whole universe?" He almost shouted it at me.

"What?" I said. His question did not even make sense.

"Well," said Eratosthenes slowly, "I have sent for the books. It will take the pages a while to retrieve them. Perhaps, while we are waiting, Psammetichus can tell us a story of his people. Then when the books arrive he can get back to whatever he ought to be doing."

A story? Did I know any stories? My mind drew a blank, and then — of course. All Egyptians love stories. Best to stick with the classics.

"Well," I said. "There was a man called Sinuhe..."

The story of Sinuhe is a story without beginning or end, and it is one of the oldest stories in the world. If it has a beginning, it starts in the court of King Ammenemes I. If I could tell you a thousand and one stories of the court of King Ammenemes, of the songs that were wrought by the harpers there beneath the star of the Ibis between sunrise and sunset - to tell you this, I would have to be one of the Gods who hung the stars in the sky, and makes the Earth move in its course.

Suffice it to this: Sinuhe was a courtier in this most famous court, serving the daughter of the King as an attendant to the Royal Wives. He was high in the ranks of those who administered the Ladies-In-Waiting, and this was an enviable position. He was a loyal servant to the throne, and a dutiful man.

But all was not well in the Kingdom. Hyenas and scorpions will fester in even the most well-ordered palace, and chaos always threatens to overcome order. One day Sinuhe, walking in the palace gardens, overheard some of his fellow courtiers plotting to overthrow the King. You see, revolution had existed within living memory, Ammenemes being the first to re-unify our country in some time. It was not unthinkable then as it is now. And may it stay unthinkable forever!

It happened that at this time the King's son, Sesostris, was in the Libyan desert, pursuing a campaign against the nomads. Thus, there was no army, and no one to stop the conspiracy from running its course. I will not speak of such evil deeds, but the King was slain, and the palace fell into mourning.

Now Sinuhe was loyal to the throne, and feared greatly the retribution that was to come upon the whole palace, for Sesostris, when he got word, turned the whole army back to punish the courtiers for their evil-doing. Sinuhe, in panic, fearing to be implicated, lost his mind, and fled the palace at once. He fled North into Lower Egypt, traveling by night and keeping to the side of the roads. He feared that if anyone saw him he would be reported and put to death - yet he was entirely an innocent man. Still, he feared, and hid on the road when he heard the call of voices. Thus he came to the boundary wall in Sinai, whose crenellations pierce the sky like teeth or broken bones. There he hid in a thicket and waited until nightfall, evaded the guard, and escaped Ægypt.

Thus Innocent Sinuhe traveled North, until he came to a rich green land, inhabited by shepherds and nomads. This land was called Yaa.

"Excuse me," said Archimedes. "Was this land Israel?"

"I don't know, sir," I said.

"If it were Israel," said Archimedes, "would not these be the ancestors of the Jews?"

"Sir, they could have been, or some other barbarian nomads of the wilderness. Whether they have any relation to the Jews I do not know for the tale I am telling you occurred thousands of years before our time."

"Then they were Philistines?"

"No, they did not settle in Canaan for many centuries later, until the rampage of the Peoples of the Sea."

"You see?" said Eratosthenes. "The memory of the Egyptians is long. Carry on, Psa."

"Very well," said Archimedes, his beady eyes settling on me with distant intensity, but as he sat back on his stool, I took it as my cue to continue:

These shepherds took Sinuhe in without a thought, they nourished him from his parched journey in the desert. He would live among them for a number of years, but such are the great qualities of this man that he rose to rank even among foreigners. The Chief of these tribes received word that Sinuhe had been an important courtier for the King of Ægypt.

He was suspicious and he asked Sinuhe what he was doing in his land, and why he had left Ægypt, whether he had been banished or fled or both. Sinuhe was still in deep fear, so he lied to their Chief, whose name was Ammunenshi, and said that he had been in King Sesostris' army that had returned from Libya, and had left and come to Yaa - better to be a deserting soldier than a conspirator! Ammunenshi was satisfied with this, and he took Sinuhe into his service. He was such a good administrator that the King even married Sinuhe to his eldest daughter.

There were many figs and grapes in Yaa, and it is said it had more wine than water. Its honey was abundant, and its oil was plentiful. All kinds of fruit were on its trees. Barley was there and emmer, and no end of cattle of all kinds. He received offerings from the local peasantry as well, for Ammunenshi had made him chief of a tribe in the most fertile part of the land of Yaa. So Sinuhe became a rich man.

He had many great adventures, fighting off the local bedouin tribes who would pilfer his land. One such barbarian even challenged him to single-handed combat. Sinuhe was less afraid of this even than the wrath of the King, and he fought the man with his longbow, and although wounded, he prevailed in the end.

But it was after this battle that Sinuhe, growing old, began to long for Ægypt. Silently he prayed to the Gods that he might be allowed to return. It seems his prayer was answered. He was recognized by a traveler, and word returned to king Sesostris that Sinuhe lived in the land of Yaa. The King sent a royal decree summoning Sinuhe back, and Sinuhe received the proclamation, terrified. He did not know if he returned he would be put to death for the conspiracy, if he was still a suspect. But eventually his longing for his homeland won out, and he left his rich and fertile farmlands and pastures to his sons and began the journey home.

At last, after much journeying, he came before King Sesotris, and fell before his might, prostrating himself. His body was trembling, for he feared even then that he was to be executed, but the King only laughed. Long ago they had rounded up the ring-leaders, and they knew Sinuhe had no part in the conspiracy. Sinuhe had grown old, and had lived among the wild men for so long he had lost the grace of civilized life. When the King summoned the Ladies-in-Waiting they did not recognize him at first, and did not believe Sesostris when he said this was the long-lost Sinuhe.

So Sinuhe was given an estate for his loyalty and courage in returning, and then he was clothed in fine linen. He was anointed with fine oil. He slept on a bed. He had returned the sand to those who dwell in it, the tree-oil to those who grease themselves with it. The King had a statue built for him, and had a stone pyramid built for him in the midst of the pyramids.

There is no commoner for whom the like has been done.

He was in the favor of the King, until the day his soul was called to the land of the dead.

The books had arrived, and the bread. Gratefully, I took a loaf from one of the servants and dipped it in a bowl of olive oil.

"What a fantastic story," said Archimedes. "I greatly enjoyed it. My favorite part was how he came back to Egypt in the end. Serve King and country — it's a good moral, like Aesop."

"What are you planning to do now, Psa?" Eratosthenes spread the folds of his toga and sat behind his desk.

"I was going to do research on Babylon, sir," I said.

"Well, then." I could see Eratosthenes was about to dismiss me but Archimedes interrupted him.

"Babylon!" he said. "Yes, that's very important. There is a book I wanted, which I found once, that I wanted to see again."

"Yes my friend?" Erathosthenes said.

"I am looking for a way to draw water upwards without heating it, and I cannot use pipes. But I remember that in the Hanging Gardens of Babylon it is said they used screws. There is a book on this in the library, somewhere. *Nineveh's Opulence,* it is called. Can you send a page to get it?"

"We have just brought many books for you here," said Eratosthenes.

"Yes, well..."

"The servants are busy preparing your repast. If you must we can get Psa to do it, since he is already going to investigate the Babylonian literature. You can fetch that for us, right Psa? If it will not be too much trouble?" He winked at me.

"Sure," I said. I excused myself, and went downstairs.

I entered the great hall of the scrolls, and searched for a scribe. Someone was there by the first gallery. I tapped him on the shoulder. It was Delphon.

"Hi," he said. "What are you looking for?"

"Delphon, I need a copy of Berossos. But also, I'm looking for a special book, called *Nineveh's Opulence*?"

"Ah," said Delphon, "From the famed library of Asorbanes."

"Sorry, who?"

"An Assyrian King," said Delphon. "Not in Berossos because he focused on Babylon, and this King ruled Nineveh, while his brother, Babylon."

"Thanks for the lesson," I said. "But can you find the book?"

"That depends," said Delphon. "Do you have those three copies of *Pinakes* everyone has been saying you pilfered?"

"For the last time," I said, "I have not been stealing from the library catalog!"

"Nevertheless, copies are missing. I can, however, take you to the Babylonian section of the archives. I think."

I decided not to bring up what the Head Librarian had said to me, or make any mention of the mysterious "Library of the Ulterior." Perhaps Delphon already knew about that. Maybe he was in on it.

"I think I remember the way, I was there last week."

"Are you sure?" said Delphon. "Let me guide you."

Delphon led me through several galleries which contained row upon row of scroll-cases. Occasionally we caught sight of scribes at work stocking and restocking the racks. Some were sorting through the tags which marked each scroll with its title. Others were carrying baskets full of papyrus scrolls at a clipped pace, delivering works to waiting scholars.

We came to a forecourt with columns, before another set of double galleries. The walls were painted in red and green. Delphon led me down a side passage into an area where a large set of stacks extended up two storeys, yet there was no obvious way to reach the upper layers.

"Here," said Delphon, "Is your Berossos." He touched a set of ten scrolls located in a basket. "Now the old address for *Nineveh* was..."

I always thought that Delphon must be using Simonides of Ceos' method; there was no other way he could keep track of the vast quantity of scrolls in the Musaion archives.

"Ah," he said. "Here it is." The basket was empty.

"So," I said, "Where is the book?"

"I think it is time," Delphon said, "That you go talk to our friend Hyginos."

I found Hyginos in a room for self-study. He was in rapt attention over a set of scrolls, staring down at them with a burning intensity.

"What are you reading?" I asked.

He looked up. "Ah, Psa," he said, smiling. "At your recommendation, I am reading a Hebrew book. It is called *The Exit*. Unfortunately, it does not seem to contain the answer to my question, of who visited my house with blood last night." He let the scroll roll shut. "How can I be of service to you?"

"I am looking for a book," I said.

"Oh good," he said, turning back to his papyrus. "I thought you would never ask."

"Sorry?"

"You have been playing dumb," he said unrolling another scroll, "for so long, I thought you might actually be made of stone. I mean, an idiot."

"I was becoming used to the library," I said.

"What does that mean?"

"It means I was keeping my options open."

"I don't like that," he said. "It means you haven't picked a side."

"Well," I said, "I'm picking one now."

"Why now?" said Hyginos. "You've had plenty of opportunities."

"The thing, Hyginos," I said, and I was speaking truthfully, "is I want the knowledge."

He smiled. "Now we're coming down to it. You're not content, are you?"

"There are some things," I said, "that I have not been able to learn."

"Corridors that were forbidden," said Hyginos. "Almost as if you wish there was *another* library."

"Yes," I said.

"Well if you want the answer to your question, you know there is only one thing you have to ask me."

I swallowed. "Hyginos," I said. "Will you take me to Sophistic Solon?"

I met them after dark. There were two of them, standing in the corridor in front of the Great Hall of the Scrolls in black robes. Was I to be initiated into something?

Then I saw I knew them. They were Orestes and Zeno.

"You're late," said Orestes.

"I had work to do," I said.

"Hm," said Zeno, "And why are you wearing a toga that says 'Official Harbourmaster' on it?"

I had not had time to change. "It's a long story."

They stared at me. I stared back.

"Well," said Orestes, "Follow us."

The doors were supposed to be bolted at night, but when they pushed on them they swung open. I stepped into the Hall of Scrolls and nearly gasped. The library was full of torches flickering in the night, spangling the scrolls with orange shadows. This was very forbidden. The risk of fire among the books was high.

Then I reminded myself that I was not in the library anymore. This was the Library of the Ulterior.

Orestes and Zeno turned and put fingers to their lips — wait, since when were they wearing bronze masks? I crept forward cautiously, ready for some strange ritual. They led me down a path through the stacks lit by blazing scrolls. The eerie light stimulated my imagination and lent the scroll cases a sinister quality. I had stopped thinking of whether we would be caught. I was thinking only of myself, and how to get out of this situation.

We came to the center of the library, the middle atrium. There were twenty of them in black robes wearing bronze and silver masks.

"Behold," said a voice I recognized as Hyginos, "does the initiate come to partake of the mysteries?"

"Indeed," said Orestes, "Kore has lost her daughter Persephone, she has gone down to Hades."

The circle cried as one, "Weep for Persephone."

"The Earth is barren," said Zeno.

"Weep for Persephone."

"Hades has her now," said Hyginos.

"Weep for Persephone."

"Does the initiate seek?" said Hyginos. I realized he was gesturing to me.

"I do," I said. "I seek Sophistic Solon."

"Weep for Persephone." This was getting creepy.

"Bring forth the sacrament," said Hyginos.

Someone whose shape I recognized as Delphon scurried forward and then brought back a bronze bowl which he set on a tripod. Hyginos, his silver mask transfigured by the light of the flames into the contorted gaze of the Rich King pointed towards the bowl. It seemed Hades himself was summoning me.

Gingerly I stepped forward towards the bowl. What was in there? A body part? A headless chicken? I could see reliefs around the rim of the bowl: a woman, grains of wheat, a skull, mourners. The circle continued to chant "Weep, weep, weep for Persephone." I gathered myself, and stepped up and peeped over the rim, what was in the bowl — Water. What was in the bowl was water. I was looking at my own reflection.

"Behold!" Hyginos shouted. "Behold Sophistic Solon!"

"Guys," I said. "Sophistic Solon... is me?"

Someone grabbed me by the neck and shoved my face down into the water. Sputtering I tried to fight him off and then another pair of hands joined and I was shoved under the surface. I flailed my arms, trying to get a hold, then these were pinned down, shit, there were too many of them. With a jolt I realized I was going to die. I saw the Atlas Mountains and the pyramid in the city of the dead before my eyes, tried to keep my lungs from taking in water, almost freed an arm, I was seeing white, THIS WAS IT.

Then suddenly they released me and I was up, coughing and shaking water from my ears, grabbing my bruised neck. "Why," I gasped, "Are you trying to kill me?"

Then I heard a thin reed-like voice I did not recognize: "Are you lot quite done initiating him into the Mysteries of Eleusis?"

"Just having some fun," said Hyginos.

"What you are doing," said the voice, "is perverting the sacraments. I assume none of you have actually entered into that mystery cult, have you?"

Silence. No one wanted to say anything.

"I thought so. Otherwise you would not act in this way."

I got up and turned around, rubbing my neck. A new figure had entered the circle, a small withered old man, wearing red robes. I could not remember ever seeing him before in my life. And like everyone else, he was wearing a mask. His mask was an image of Dionysus.

"Greetings," said the man. "You must be Psammetichus. I have heard about you."

"Can I ask who you are?" I said, still a bit irate from the general deception.

"You may call me Solon. Solon the Sophist. For like my namesake, I too am a poet."

"So you are real," I said.

He ignored this. "You have come here with a question."

"Yes," I said. "I am looking for a book."

He shook his head. "No," he said. "That is not correct. You have come here looking for a Book."

I stood up. "Who are you? Why are you doing this?"

"Hmm," said Sophistic Solon. "Are you one who loves wisdom? Are you one who loves knowledge? And are you prepared to say those are one and the same?"

I thought for a second. "Yes," I said at last. The brothers around the circle laughed. "I understand there is a philosophical war." That shut them up.

"A philosophical war?" said Solon. "There are flames and there are shadows. The war over our philosophy is just a shadow of a greater war, a war that occurs throughout the entire world: the Creation War."

"The world is at war?" I said.

"So the Prophet Zoroaster teaches," said Sophistic Solon.

"Then what are we doing here?"

"Our part," the poet said. "We are keeping the flame alive, by feeding the shadow."

"I am looking for a book from the East."

"Yes, *Nineveh's Opulence.* I heard." Solon paced around the circle and looked distractedly down into the bowl, whose water was still rippling.

"It's about the Hanging Gardens of Babylon."

Sophistic Solon turned and looked at me. His eyes through the mask were like points of black light. "You know that the gardens are not in Babylon? They are in Nineveh."

"Come again?" I said. "Then why does everyone call them the Hanging Gardens of *Babylon*?"

"Because Herodotus could not tell the difference. And he never went there."

"Can you find me that book?" I said.

"I can find you that book," said Solon. "But that is not the Book that you are looking for."

"What are you talking about?"

"There is a book you are looking for, of which you are unaware."

"And which book is that?" I said.

"The Book of Thoth."

I laughed out loud. "Oh, don't be ridiculous."

"Hm?" said Solon. He looked at me confused.

I was still laughing, I could not help it. "This is some Greek nonsense. There is no one 'Book of Thoth.' Try as you might Solon, it remains even as it was for your predecessor, despite all this opulence: 'You Greeks are like children. There is not an old man among you.' "

"What do you mean?" said Sophistic Solon. "And why do you speak to an elder in this way?"

"Manetho estimates," I said, "that there are more than 30,000 books of Thoth, but that is a low estimate. Don't you see? A 'Book of Thoth' is just a book in a temple library. There are certain canonical texts, but the actual scriptures vary from nome to nome."

"I thought I heard once," Delphon said, "that there were 42 books of Thoth? One for each nome?"

"This is true in most places," I said, "As it is true in my home city of Sais. But the actual number is different in every nome, even every temple, and although there are certain liturgical similarities you can assume that each temple has, well — " I gestured to Solon, "even if you had an index of them all you would never be able to say how many or what they were, the index would constantly be growing. And the index would be as old as time. These books are eternal."

"Nevertheless," said Solon, "I assure you that this Book exists."

I stopped. "Who are you," I said, "oh defender of Eleusis, to say anything about my own religion?"

"I know that this book exists," said Sophistic Solon, "because I have it in the Library of the Ulterior."

Solon led me to a part of the upper gallery I had never been to before. It was above the main atrium, facing inwards, and abutted a dead end. Contained here were war reports and property records dating back to Alexander's conquests. Two racks from the end we stopped.

Sophistic Solon reached into a recession, groping, and I saw the bland, smiling face of Dionysus gaze eerily upon me. Then he pulled out something from within the rack: a scroll evidently very old. He handed it to me.

It was a book written in demotic, called "The Book of Hermopolis." I unrolled it.

And Re confronts Apep, the world serpent,
Wadjet's shadow, the being of Isfet.
The ba-souls of Re fall down on their hands.
In the underworld, beneath Hermopolis, he confronts
him.

For Hermopolis is the center of the world.

"Well?" said Solon.

"This is a different genre of our literature," I said. "And it has nothing to do with Thoth."

"Are you sure?" he said.

"Yes! It does not even have anything to do with the theology of Thoth's city, the city from which it purports to come."

"Read it again," said Sophistic Solon.

I sighed, and unrolled it the whole way, starting at the beginning. Then I stopped suddenly. Was it my imagination, or had the book changed in my hands? It had been old before, but now the papyrus was new. It was not written in demotic anymore, it was written in hieroglyphs.

"What is this?" I said. "How are you doing this?"

"Just read it," said Sophistic Solon.

I looked at the first line.

There are 8 kinds of infinity.

A thrill went through me. "Greek man," I said. "Where did you get this?"

Was Solon smiling behind his mask? I could not tell. Dionysus was.

I held up the scroll. "This is forbidden."

"The Library of the Ulterior," said Solon, "is where

we find all forbidden knowledge."

4 are male, and 4 are female.

"Who are you," I hissed at him, and I put my hands on my hips, "to chastise them for the mockery of your Eleusinian Mysteries, when you have not been initiated into the Ogdoad, and yet — you make a mockery of it here?"

"You are holding," said Solon, "The Book of Thoth."

"There is no one Book of Thoth!" I shouted.

"Be careful," said Solon. "Like you said, it's not my religion, but if I were you I would not want to offend a God."

For Thoth keeps the ledger of eternity.
He it is who causes Re to emerge
From the Cosmic Egg.
He it is, who, allied with the Moon
Causes the revolutions of the Sun.

I had never read anything quite like this before. Ever.

"Can I...take this book with me when I leave the Library of the Ulterior?"

"What book?" said Sophistic Solon. "Were you holding a book?"

With a shock I realized there was nothing in my hands.

He leaned in close to me. "A word to the wise," he whispered. "Do not be too greedy when it comes to knowledge. It scares the Gods away."

"But Sophistic Solon," I said, "where did you get such a book?"

He started laughing, a low, long chuckle. "My child. Do you think I am the author of the Library of the Ulterior?"

Somehow, by night, Delphon was able to locate *Nineveh's Opulence* for me; when I asked him why he could do it in the Ulterior Library but not during normal business hours he simply said, "Some knowledge can only be found by seeking it in the right way."

We agreed to meet again in a fortnight and reopen the Library of the Ulterior. The rest of them seemed to like me now. Some of them even invited me to attend a play with them at sunrise. I refused, politely — Greek pageants are not my favorite. Hyginos refused as well. "One of my cows is coming down sick," he said. "I'm going to be busy in the morning."

We parted, and I went back to my cell, mind whirling. The Book of Thoth? I suppose you could say it was heresy, or perversion. I can only think what my elders back home would say. And yet, the book I held had *seemed* Egyptian, even though it was like no other Egyptian book I had ever read…

I went back to my cell and shut the door. I turned to take my toga off, and came face to face with the ghost.

It was standing in the corner, staring at me. Its eyes were like pinpricks of black light. It was holding a book.

"Please," I said. "Please, do not take my ka!"

The ghost was opening and closing its mouth.

"Is your akh displeased? Is your akh displeased? If so, I will find your resting place and leave offerings for you. I swear it. Just please, please, do not take my life."

The ghost raised a finger and began to point at me.

"Please," I said. "By Anubis I have not sinned, I have been merciful!" I thought of the headless chicken. "Except upon one man — but he was a foreigner!" I figured that foreigners did not count. Let the reader pause here. If there is any one lesson to be drawn from my life it is this: when you are standing before the tribunal which judges your heart, and you do *not* want your soul to be fed to the devourer, equivocation is a bad idea.

The ghost pointed right at my heart.

You will remember me.

I did not so much hear it as feel it. Then he was gone.

You will remember me? What did that mean? I glanced around the room, checking the corners with my hands. Then, deciding I would be unable to sleep in darkness I lit an oil lamp. I removed the toga and prepared for bed. You will remember me…what?

Then, halfway between sleep and waking, I understood. It was like Manetho says. The soul both transmigrates, and it abides.

The next day I brought Archimedes the book he had asked for. He was in a room above the forecourt, with a rooftop terrace where he could view the movements of the planets. A page led me inside to the center of the room, where a giant machine with a series of gears and dials was sitting, made from green-gold brass.

"What is this thing?" I breathed.

"A calculating machine," said Archimedes, descending from the roof terrace. "Like an abacus. Very special and rare."

"Is it..." I paused. "Is it a sphere?"

"It is a kind of orrery, yes," said Archimedes, "like we were talking about the other day. I am also an expert on making these things. But my skill does not compare with one man, Apollodorus of Rhodes. I am very excited about this. For years I have been attempting to procure one of his contraptions and have it sent to Syracuse; unfortunately when I finally acquired the funds, the ship that was carrying it sank off the island of Antikythera. Luckily," he said, "I was overjoyed to find Eratosthenes had also commissioned one from him."

"So these gears make calculations?" I said. "How?"

"It is too long to explain," said Archimedes. "But here, you are a student of mechanics, and the scribes have finished copying my book. Let us make a trade: a book for a book." He handed me a scroll. The tag on it bore the title *On Sphere-Making.* Suddenly, I had the otherworldly sense, a tingling on my still-bruised neck, that this book also belonged to the Library of the Ulterior.

"Thank you for acquiring *Nineveh's Opulence*," he said. "It may interest you to know that I learned something yesterday."

"Did you, sir?"

"Yes. I spoke with a priest at the Serapaeum who informed me the water screw was invented here in Egypt and taken by the Assyrians when they built their gardens. He showed me stone inscriptions to that effect which proved it."

"Well, of course," I said. "All Babylonian knowledge originally comes from Egypt; our society is much older."

"Spoken by an Egyptian. I do not know if that is true, but I myself have kept to Herodotus and left Berossos and Manetho for the historians."

"And yet," I said, "you say these words on Egyptian soil. Surely that speaks for itself. There must be some reason which draws you Greeks back here."

"It sounds like you could work at the Serapaeum yourself."

"I would rather serve *Osiris* at the temple in Memphis, sir."

"You Egyptians are always combining and merging Gods," said Archimedes. "What's the difference?"

"The difference, sir, is that we do it elegantly."

Archimedes laughed. "Luckily I am not a theologian. But listen to this about the water screw. According to this priest it was invented by Imhouthes for irrigation, and first used to great effect to fill the lake which surrounded the Pyramid of Cheops."

"Sorry, invented by whom?" I said, heart racing.

Archimedes looked at me with disbelief. "Imhouthes," he said. "The sage Imhouthes. The most famous Egyptian *ever*."

I was silent.

"You are the worst Egyptian I have ever met. Why do you pretend to be a patriot? Imhouthes practically invented your religion."

"No," I said, "I know who that is."

"I should think so," said Archimedes. When I did not say anything else he said, "Something's spooked you then. I've broken some religious vow."

"Perhaps we can talk more about mechanics," I said.

"Certainly," he said. "But why don't you study that

book first? I've got things to do, and afterwards you can ask me some educated questions."

I left the room, and went back down to the scroll rooms, but my heart was not in the work. My mind was in the Atlas Mountains, standing before the sage Imhouthes, at the gate to the City of the Dead.

A few weeks later, I met Sumethres and Osarseph at one of the ale-houses I used to go to. They were very drunk.

"What, you again?" said Osarseph as I came up to the long table. "Haven't you gotten lost in your books yet?"

"One day," said Sumethres, "he will drown in them. They will shut him up in there and he will never come back. Like in a tomb."

They made a cry and banged their bowls of wine together.

"What's got you two in such a good mood?" I said.

Sumethres leaned forward. "Do you remember Hyginos?" he whispered.

"Yes, I see him every day," I said. But I knew what he meant. Two of his cows had died, which was a great misfortune. Even for a rich man like him, that was a lot of money.

"But you see," said Osarseph, draining his bowl. "It's spreading."

"What?" I said.

"It infected his neighbors, and then it infected some bedouin herders who had been keeping their animals in that abandoned building."

I put my head in my hands. "By the Gods."

"So you see," said Sumethres, "already it is spreading around half the city. Cows are going sick everywhere, and people are starting to talk of a plague."

"Like in *Exodus*," said Osarseph.

"What can we do?" I said.

"Pray to the angel of the Lord," said Osarseph. "Repent from your heathen religion." He hiccupped. "I told you that sacrilege would come to a bad end..."

"You seemed pretty gung-ho when we were actually doing the deed."

"Ignore him," said Sumethres. "He's been saying that all night. The bigger problem is whether it can be traced to Hyginos' cows."

"Are they aware?" I said.

"Well the magistrate is investigating."

"The magistrate?"

Osarseph nodded. "Hyginos made an official complaint to the office of the King. First he blamed the Jews."

"Oh..." I said. "Sorry..."

Osarseph waved a hand. "So they summoned the rabbis and the King was made aware this was not a Jewish thing. Then Hyginos claimed someone was working black magic against him."

"Which is true," said Sumethres.

"We just don't know," said Osarseph, "Whether he has made the connection between the death of his cows and the so-called curse. It is just a matter of time but nothing in public has been said about it."

"However," said Sumethres, "last I checked the magistrate's investigation was still open."

"Meanwhile cows are dying all over the city."

"Correctamundo." Osarseph gestured for more wine.

"Sumet," I said.

"What? It's not the first time I talked you into something. It won't be the last."

"Don't you understand though?" I said. "I work with Hyginos."

"If you call that paper-pushing you do work."

"That isn't the point - I see him all the time. I am in great danger."

"What?" said Sumet. "No one would ever suspect you of fraternizing with Egyptians. You're too Greekified."

"It's true," said Osarseph, burping. "He's the Greekest Egyptian I know."

"So no one has any reason to think you would actually put a spell on one of your fellow scholars. Besides, nobody saw you there, right?"

I shook my head no.

"So relax. You have nothing to worry about."

That night, I met my brethren in the Library of the Ulterior. I brought the mask Sumet had pilfered for me before: Tragedy. We came together in the atrium, at midnight. A waxing gibbous moon was shining through the skylight. We said little, exchanging mostly gestures and glances. Then, we saw a light bobbing in the stacks, coming closer toward us, and Sophistic Solon emerged in the mask of Dionysus, carrying an oil lamp.

"What are your questions?" he said.

They were many. Someone wanted the original account of the Trojan War. Solon spent a long time mulling this over before giving off a list of volumes from many countries, which seemed unrelated. *Book of the Philistines. Aretalogy of the Orphic Mysteries. History of Thracia.* But these volumes in their nonsensical order were accepted with a bow, and a word of gratitude. Then the questioner vanished into the stacks.

Then Sophistic Solon came to me. "What are you searching for, Egyptian?"

I looked at him.

"Would you like to see again the book I showed you last time?"

"No," I said. "Tell me about Imhouthes."

"You mean Asklepios," he said.

"No, I mean Imhouthes."

"Very well," said Solon. "Follow me."

He led me to a long set of stacks which went off down a dark corridor.

"This is the section of medicine."

"But Imhouthes was not just a doctor."

"Yet like Asklepios he invented medicine."

"But he is not Asklepios."

"No, he is Imhouthes."

He pulled a scroll out from a basket marked "History of Medicine" and unrolled it before me.

Asklepios was the son of Apollo and the princess Corona. The midwife Lachesis attended at his birth. Apollo named the child after the name he had for Corona, aegile. He was...

"This is exactly what I told you not to find for me," I said.

"Hm," said Solon. "We'll put that back then."

"Why do you Greeks understand nothing? Imhouthes was a great Doctor, but he is not just the God of medicine."

"Perhaps your better question is, how does a man become a God?"

I paused. "Perhaps."

"There are several ways," said Solon, turning and walking down the stacks. I followed. "One is the way of Name."

"The way of Name?"

"Through great deeds. Automatically. You will hear now that throughout Alexander's Empire, already, just three generations after his death, he is revered as a God. His name is worshiped as a God on account of his great deeds. This is the way of Name."

"Not here in Alexandria," I said.

"Here we worship Serapis," said Solon, "But why do you think so many pilgrims are coming to his tomb at the center of this city? Already, he is a God."

"What are the other ways?"

"Ask the gymnosophists," said Solon.

"What?"

"Ask the gymnosophists. The naked wise-ones. They live in the East, in the valley of the Indus River, but Alexander brought back many of the scholars from their great school, Taxila."

"I do not go to the East. I am an Egyptian man, with an Egyptian question, about an Egyptian sage."

"But you see, now again, you are looking for the Book of Thoth."

"Why do you keep talking about a non-existent book?"

"A book which you held in your hands last time."

"I do not know what I held."

Solon turned to me. "Then I cannot answer your question."

"You cannot?"

"I cannot answer your question because it is no longer a question for the Library of the Ulterior. You already know the answer."

"Do I?"

"Yes. You already know the answer of how a man becomes a God better than me, for you are an Egyptian, and you already know that Egypt is the birthplace of all religion."

He left and walked away, and I was standing in the dark stacks alone. Did I already know the answer?

There are two forms of time. The soul both transmigrates, and it abides.

Back in my cell, I dreamed of the City of the Dead. But this time, the City was not in the Atlas Mountains. The City was just over the river, across from the city of Memphis. I looked upon the pyramid of King Zoser, its stairway leading to the stars. I looked upon the akh of King Zoser, and the akh was glowing with light.

"What are the parts of the soul?" said a voice. I turned, and saw my ghost.

"Are you Imhouthes?" I said.

"No," said the ghost. "I am one of his assistants."

"What are the parts of the soul?"

"Or the akh," said my ghost.

"The akh is the whole soul," I said, "and the work is already complete."

"Yet the work can fail, and the akh can fail to reach immortality," said my ghost.

"Both are true," I said.

"Why not just end it now, Psammetichus? You are already immortal."

"It is my ba which says that," I said. "Because it wants to wine in the Land of the Dead."

"But I am your akh," said my ghost.

"If you are my akh, then the argument is already completed. As you have just said, the work can fail, even though we are immortal. The soul both transmigrates, and it abides."

"Is the work in the tomb? Is the work in the incantation?"

"The magic completes the work but the magic is not the work," I said.

"Yet Heka is the word of binding," said my ghost.

"This is true," I said.

"Is Heka Logos?" asked my ghost.

"Now you are being ridiculous," I said. "You are making a translation from Egyptian into Greek. It is as ridiculous as saying that Asklepios is Imhouthes."

"Why do you find this ridiculous?" said my akh. "You, who already know that all Gods are one?"

"Wait," I said. "I'm not dead yet. How are you, my akh, able to talk to me, before my ka and my ba have been reunited?"

"Clearly," said my akh, "Someone has been leaving you a lot of offerings after you die."

"So you see," I said to Orestes in the gymnasium, "In fact this Imhouthes was a real person. He built the first pyramid that you see in this country, to the west of Memphis."

Orestes picked up a practice discus and threw it. "I thought that is how all the Gods were born. They were all once men, and then over time, their stories took on the character of legends."

Zeno snorted. He was lounging against the far wall. "He knows nothing. How do you explain the emergence of a historical religion, such as the religion of Dionysus?"

"He came from the East," said Orestes, leveling another discus. "Perhaps Dionysus was a real person in the East, perhaps in Persia."

"Shows what this man knows about the Persian religions," said Zeno, laughing.

"I know nothing about Persia, or this sage Zoroaster," I said.

"Neither do I," said Zeno. "But I know they are not like a bacchanal!"

"Idiots," said Orestes. "That is not the point. The point is, what are the Gods if they are not men, in principle? Otherwise why do they bear the images of men?"

"Orestes," I said, "Do you have a religion?"

"If it was allowed," said Zeno, "I think Orestes would be an Epicurean."

"If it was allowed?" I said.

Hush, hush, Zeno mouthed, jerking his head towards the far door. Eratosthenes had just entered the gym.

"So anyways, this Imhouthes," I said. "He invents hydraulics, mathematics, stone architecture, medicine, he even reforms the hieroglyphs."

"I heard it was his wife who did the last part," said Eratosthenes.

"What?" I said.

"Oh, just something I heard once from an old priest in Hermopolis. Carry on."

"They still worship his cult in the Metropolis of the Dead. Beyond Memphis, at Zoser's funerary complex. Pilgrims bring offerings of the ibis bird there."

"Yes," said Orestes, "I was wondering about that. Why do you Egyptians keep up that horrid practice anyways?"

"What?" I said.

"Of mummifying the animals." He threw his disc. "It's

abhorrent. Couldn't you just sacrifice them like everyone else?"

"It's... complicated."

"The Gods will hear the sacrifice anyways," said Orestes.

"Says the man," said Eratosthenes, "who is not even sure he believes in the Gods."

"You laugh at my skepticism, teacher, but I at least have respect for ritual form, and for... hygiene."

"Did someone say my name?" said Hyginos, entering.

"We're having a debate about mummification," said Zeno.

"Ew," said Hyginos. "Why?"

"I don't know," said Zeno. "What's new with you?"

"Well, my last cow has died." Everyone gasped.

"No," said Eratosthenes. "That is horrible. Such misfortune. And has anyone been able to tell the cause of this plague?"

"I have been consulting the Oracles," Hyginos preened himself, in that way he did when he wanted maximum attention from a crowd.

"And?" we prompted.

"Supposedly I have been the victim of ill will from some members of the city's population, and justice lies in the next-of-kin."

"Well that's cryptic," said Eratosthenes.

"You know oracles," said Orestes. "They need to preserve their credibility. The best thing to do is to supply an answer that can fulfill any question you have."

"I need someone to come to my house," said Hyginos.

"Why?" said Eratosthenes.

"To get the bad influences away," he said.

Eratosthenes shook his head, smiling. "It does not work like that."

"All the same," he said. "Psa, I was wondering if you might come. I need an Egyptian, and you are the only Egyptian I actually like."

I swallowed. Was this a trap? Everyone was looking at me. "Sure," I said. "I'll come."

I did not have a chance to get away. Hyginos and I were walking down the street together, while he chatted airily about the plague. I was searching passers-by, desperately hoping to see someone I knew, someone I could signal to *get Sumethres quick* but they were all strangers. We were walking through the Royal Quarter.

"So apparently," he was saying, "I spoke with the magistrate last Sunday, and he said to me that this plague that has been spreading around the city? My cows were the first reported case of it. Isn't that extraordinary?"

"Yeah," I said. "It is."

"It has been affecting the Greek and Jewish neighborhoods," he said. "But none of the Egyptian cows have come down with it! Conniving, right? No offense of course, Psa."

"Oh, none taken," I said. "I live in the Musaion."

"Right!" said Hyginos. "You're basically a Greek.

That's why I like you." He threw his arm over my shoulder. "You even read our philosophy."

"So Hyginos," I said, trying not to look as uncomfortable as I felt, "what exactly do you want me to do at your house?"

"Tell me if there was a curse, and in the name of what God. You can do that right, with your Egyptian powers?"

Where do they get these things?

"Hyginos," I said. "I am not a soothsayer, and do not possess the ability to read spells by sight."

"Nonsense," he said. "Anyways, you're better off an interpreter of magic than I am, I'll tell you that. Besides, this is my interpretation of the Oracle's proclamation: justice lies in the next of kin. Which means I need an Egyptian to decode this riddle for me. And seeing as I don't know any Egyptians other than you, you'll have to do. Besides," he lowered his voice, "you owe me one. I introduced you to Sophistic Solon."

I could not argue with that. And unfortunately, Hyginos lived much closer to the Musaion than any of my alehouses, so we did not encounter anyone I knew on the street. We came to his house and I found myself standing in front of a small portico, with a set of double doors embossed with many colored triangles.

"Welcome to my abode," said Hyginos. "This is the door."

"The door?" I said. It looked different in the daytime. "It's quite striking."

"Beautiful isn't it? Imagine my face when I came out that morning and found the threshold and the door frame painted in blood, the body of a vile chicken laying out here! Isn't that horrid? Although I suppose, you're Egyptian, so you don't have anything against dead animals, do you?"

"I prefer them mummified," I said.

"Quite right, it was not even a mummified dead chicken — see, even an Egyptian — now come here," he gestured (could he be more insufferable and how screwed am I), "see, there is blood caked to this wood here. I have tried to scrub it all off but it has not gone away. What do you make of that?"

"It's blood," I said.

"Quite right," he said. "Come inside."

I knew that, if I valued my life, it was wise for me to not go into the house. However, I also knew that if I did anything suspicious, Hyginos would go to the magistrate, and I would be drawn and quartered for starting a plague that had destroyed half the city's livestock. The truth is, neither of these things influenced my decision to go through that door at all. On the cursed threshold of Hyginos' house, the only image that came to me was the troglodyte, and the round window, and the infinite hallway stretching off behind it. A desire rose in me, a curiosity and a sense of the mysterious, and I almost forgot that I was a suspect in a case that had caused massive property damage. I wanted to see the inside of Hyginos' house for its own sake, and it is this desire that set me more in the order of Sophistic Solon than any other.

So, I entered.

And I found myself face to face with the goddess Athena in the foyer, staring at me intently.

"Do you like her?" said Hyginos. "She is the goddess of your city."

"You mean Neith," I said.

"Yes," said Hyginos. "You know I have always admired the priests of Sais, Psa. Ever since I was a little boy." Behind the statue of the Goddess was a mirror, whose angle he adjusted until it aligned with - another mirror, and I had the curious sensation of looking into the sky. "Have you ever visited the Labyrinth at Crocodilopolis?"

"No," I said. "But I know it. It is sacred to King Ammenemes III."

"I don't know anything about that, I don't read your history. But what a labyrinth, Psa! Oh, if only you could see it. You must go there someday, promise me. It covers two storeys and contains three thousand rooms. Half of them are above ground, half of them are below, and they are filled with mummified crocodiles." He shivered. "Ugh!"

"What does this have to do with anything?" I said.

"I was so inspired by this labyrinth when I went there as a youth, that when I inherited this house from my father,

I decided to make it a labyrinth in imitation of that one, in memory of the city of the crocodiles. Of course, I lacked the space to build 3,000 rooms, so you know what I used?"

"What?" I said.

"Mirrors!" he said, clapping his hands like a child. "Mirrors, yes, so I could live in infinity! Let me show you." He scurried off down a dark corridor, and picked up a lamp. He struck flint and steel half a dozen times, lit a small taper, then proceeded down the hall. I found myself following him, the eyes of Athena on my back.

The colors of the hall were black, ochre, and pink. They were painted in great plaster bands, and the floor was a mosaic made to represent the sea. Hyginos went through a beaded curtain at the end. I followed him, and entered an impossible room.

Stairs. That is the first thing I saw. Stairs in all directions. It seemed that the floor before me turned, and marched forwards, turning into circular stairs which led to the ceiling. Next to me, I saw the same set of stairs descending into the Earth. There were columns, coming from the ceiling like stalactites, but they never reached the floor. Equally, there were stalagmite columns that never reached the ceiling. There was a single window in the far wall, but the window was not round.

Hyginos was standing on the stairs that descended into the ground. "Come," he said, beckoning with the candle. "Enter my labyrinth. See if it compares to the city of your ancient Kings."

"Hyginos," I said, "Where does this lead?"

"Down," he said, giggling. "Down."

This was getting odd. "Hyginos," I said. "I fail to see how this will help me determine the nature of the curse on your door frame."

"Oh, please," he said. "You are my guest, allow me to host you!" He was halfway down the steps now.

An even worse feeling was settling into my stomach. "Is it alright with you if I stay up here?" No, he would insist -

"Of course not, I insist!" His voice was echoing off some great chamber, and I could see shadows from his light dimly flickering on the steps.

I decided not to be rude and gingerly followed him down. Too far down. How could these stairs be here? It was as though we were marching down under the street outside. Ahead of me I could see Hyginos backlit, like an icon, brandishing the lamp before his stooped frame.

It struck me then that he might try to kill me. For a moment it was crystal clear. He must have found out I was with the crowd who cursed his doorstep. This was a ruse, and he was taking me down into a crypt, no witnesses. I was about to flee before reflection caught me: it was unlikely he would suspect - could troglodytes even talk? - and just like in the gymnasium, the best thing for me was to play along. All the same, I swept my eyes across the passage, looking for potential weapons. Nothing.

Suddenly, the stairs ended, and opened into a large cavern. In the center of the cavern was a giant brazier on a tripod, and Hyginos was standing next to it, lighting it from his open lamp, which was resting on the ground next to him. Curiously, it seemed to mirror the room we had just left: stalactites lowering like uncomplete columns, barely missing the rising stalagmites.

"Wow," I said. "Did you inherit this too?"

"This," said Hyginos, "is the shadow of my labyrinth."

"What does that mean?"

"The shadow," said Hyginos, grinning, "and the flame."

The brazier sprung to light, striking every corner of the cave at once. Suddenly the natural face of the rock was glittering, revealing the intricate facets of the stalagmites. It was as though the stars had been locked under the Earth. On the wall was a relief of a giant God I could not identify. A Greek one, obviously minor - not Zeus...below his feet was an opening identical to the one we had come down, containing another set of stairs going up. No, it was a mirror of polished stone, perfectly aligned, that looked as if —

"Would you like some wine?" said Hyginos.

"Gladly," I said. "So you said you built a labyrinth from mirrors?"

He had bent behind a stalactite and was tugging at an enormous krater.

"Hey, do you want some help with that?"

"No," he huffed. "I. Got it." He threw a stone lid aside and dipped a pewter vessel into a vat of wine.

"Do you...have any servants?"

"Hm? No," said Hyginos. "No, I don't have any servants."

"But you said you inherited the house."

"I did," said Hyginos. "My Father liberated all the slaves. I mean the freedmen. He freed them."

"Oh, really?" I said. "All of them? That's very generous of him. But he didn't keep anyone in employ?"

"It's rude to inquire about someone's source of income, Psa."

Rather oblique. "I didn't know money was tight," I said. "I was just innocently..."

"It's not tight," said Hyginos, thrusting a cup of wine into my hand. "You're getting ruder."

"Sorry," I said.

"It's fine. Do you like it? My labyrinth?"

"I don't feel like I have really seen it yet," I said. "Is that a mirror?" I pointed to the far passage.

"Yes," he said. "The first one I built actually."

"And which God is that?"

"Ganymede," said Hyginos. "The cup-bearer of Zeus."

"Huh," I said. "That's an interesting choice." I sipped the wine. It was pungent, and bitter. It was close to vinegar. "Hyginos," I said. "This wine."

"Has it gone bad?" he said. "My apologies."

"You insisted I come down here on the basis of your hospitality."

"I'm terribly sorry," he said. He looked mortified.

At that exact moment a bird flew down into the cave, carrying a scroll. It flew over our heads, weaving through the glittering stalactites, coming so close I could feel the rush of wind on my scalp. Then it flew past, straight for the second opening. It hit the mirror, and fell dead. "Huh," I said. "What was that?"

"Probably a message," said Hyginos. He threw his cup to the ground with disdain, and started picking across the ground towards it. I followed him.

"A message from whom?"

"Who do you think?"

The bird was a falcon, and there was a scroll of papyrus tied to it with red cord. "Woah," I said. "That is a very sacred bird. This is a bad omen." I said a prayer under my breath, blessing the ba-souls of Horus.

"Hmm," said Hyginos abstractedly. "What God is this again in your religion?" He cut the scroll from the bird's talons and unrolled it. "Yes," he said. "It's from Sophistic Solon." He scrutinized it.

"Can I see it?" I said.

"It's not that interesting," he said. He handed it to me. Written on the scroll were a series of spells invoking Agathodaimon. Spells to enchant the sky, and bind the daimon of another man to your will...

"What is this?" I said "I don't understand. How do you know this is a message from Solon?"

"This is his symbol," said Hyginos, pointing to the lower corner of the scroll. A snake biting its own tail, with an arrow going through it. In red ink.

"Huh," I said. "Almost like a hieroglyph. Why is he sending this to us?"

"I don't know," said Hyginos. "This is very typical."

I had more questions, but I knew better than to ask who Sophistic Solon was at this point. "Why is this man like this? Why does he always play with riddles?"

"For him, I think, it is the nature of his philosophy."

"His philosophy is to make us confused?"

"He wants to provoke us into having the revelations we could not have otherwise. To think the unthinkable. Know the unknowable."

"And that always has to involve the forbidden," I said.

"Precisely," said Hyginos. "If you are looking for what is unknown, you will not find it in what is acceptable."

"But that is dangerous," I said.

"Yes," said Hyginos. "Solon is a philosopher, but he is also a magician."

"I could tell that," I said, thinking of the transforming scroll.

"Yes, but you have not found out what form of magic you practice yet. Or, I don't know, you Egyptians invented magic, so maybe you are practicing some form of it we don't know."

"What form is it for you?"

"For me?" said Hyginos. "Isn't it obvious? Illusions." He gestured to the cavern. "My labyrinth."

"So, wait," I said. "None of this is real?"

"You tell me," he said.

I went over and tapped a stalagmite. It felt solid. It seemed like rock. "This feels real."

"Well," said Hyginos. "Do you know?"

What a strange question. "I mean, I think we are beyond knowing at this point. Or even demonstration."

"Let me put it another way," said Hyginos. "Do you believe that the Hyperboreans are real?"

"What does that have to do with anything? I guess I believe in Hyperboreans."

"But you have never seen one."

"I have never seen a lot of things. But I have just seen your stalagmite, here. And touched it."

"That bird saw a passage out of this cavern."

"And then it rammed into the mirror there and now it is dead. Presto."

"But in the moment before it rammed into the mirror," said Hyginos, "the bird believed in Hyperboreans."

"I am really having trouble seeing how Herodotus comes into all this."

"But you see," said Hyginos, "Illusion is all about

seeming and being, and the distance between the two. No matter which of the five senses you rely on there are always appearances. And any one of them can be fooled." He picked up an unlit torch and swung it towards the stalagmite as though it were a sword. It swished through like milk and water. I stared. Then I tapped the stalagmite again. It was perfectly solid.

"How?" I said.

"I already told you, silly," he said. "Mirrors."

Hyginos went to the mirror on the far side of the cavern and lifted it up. Behind it, there actually was a passage, a small, round, grimy hole. "Come on," he said, and pulled himself inside.

I followed him, and lifted up the obsidian mirror, round as Athena's shield. The grotto behind it was barely large enough for me to crouch in, and pulling myself up, I found I had to half-hop, half crawl. There was barely any light at the far end, and I found myself getting distressed, thinking I might get shut down in the ground, when I tumbled out into a perfectly hexagonal chamber. The walls of the chamber were covered in frescos of ships and fish, and it was incredibly tall, at least three stories, like a tower. Hyginos was already sitting about two stories up, his feet dangling from a small window, holding a bundle of rope in his hands.

"I will only let you proceed if you answer three riddles," he said.

"Hyginos," I said. "This is very strange. I came here to diagnose the curse on your household."

"Yes, but I like you," he said. "So I decided to show you around."

"But, Hyginos. This place is infinite."

"That is because you cannot tell the difference between reality and appearances."

"So what is this, some kind of sadistic lesson?"

"There's no use whining," said Hyginos. "This time I get to be the sphinx! The first riddle is: *I rise to the sky, I make eyes cry, I make lungs sigh: I signal destruction to be nigh.*"

"Sphinxes don't tell riddles," I said. "They guard the -
"

"Yes, yes," said Hyginos, waving his hand. "Enough of your Egyptian hair-splitting."

"I thought this was about truth and falsehood."

"Absolutely not," said Hyginos. "You're still not getting it. It's about reality and appearances."

I thought for a second, but the riddle was easy enough, he had given me plenty of clues to get it in those four lines. "Smoke," I said.

"Correct!" he said. "Because where there is smoke, there is fire. That is the first lesson in appearances and reality. Second riddle: *From the Roof of the World, to the Pits of Tartarus, over the Circles of the Sun, I contain all things.*"

"Ha! That is too easy," I said. "Because it is an Egyptian saying translated into Greek. The Egg, the Egg of Orpheus."

"Well done. Final riddle: *By Fire I come one way. By Water I come two. By Air I come three. By Earth I come not.*"

"Empedocles," I said. "This is about Empedocles."

"Oh Wow," said Hyginos. "Close."

"Empedocles throwing himself into Mount Etna to prove he is a God," I said.

"Nope," said Hyginos. "Guess again."

"A bronze sandal."

"You're just guessing things associated with Empedocles. Think about it. How does his missing shoe come one way by Fire but three ways by Air? It would be one way by Fire and Air, and none by Water at all."

"Now *you're* hair-splitting," I said.

"And you're still not getting it. Try again."

"Hyginos, can't you just give up this charade and let the ladder down?"

"Not until you get the third riddle right."

"I will just leave," I said. "I did not sign up for this." I turned to look for the passage I had come through, but suddenly could not find the hole. I felt around the walls with my hands, looking for the illusion but it was all perfectly smooth plaster. "Hyginos," I said, "will you stop doing this? This is creepy." He was laughing.

"Guess the third riddle," he said.

I thought. I paced around the chamber, while Hyginos dangled his feet above, humming. Then - of course. It was simple. And close to my first guess.

"Volcano," I said. "The Forge of Hephaestus. Because when the Fire-Mountain erupts it comes out as lava, as Fire, which takes a second form when it solidifies in Water, and two more as Pumice and Ash in Air."

"Well reasoned," said Hyginos. "My prince, you may ascend." He threw the rope down the wall and I saw it was woven as a ladder. He stepped away from the window, and I began to climb up. Halfway up the wall I heard a tremendous clamor and I almost lost my footing on the rungs and fell to the ground. I grabbed with my left hand and clung: the ladder swung suddenly halfway around the room. I was dangling, like a pendulum, trying not to move too much to slowly swing back. The sound came again. It was a clarion call. Hyginos was...blowing a horn? He stuck his curly-haired head out the window and grinned at me. "Trumpeting your ascent!"

"You are so weird. A little help here?"

He disappeared again and seemed to tug on one of the ropes. I swung back to underneath the window, a bit further up now, righted myself, and pulled myself up the last few rungs.

When I got to the window, I found Hyginos was not there. Instead, there was a long hallway, perfectly straight, extending into the far distance. At the end was a doorway

116

glowing with light. I stepped forward and instantly rammed my head into a full-body mirror at a tilt. Ow.

I turned to the right and saw the same passage extending into the same distance with the same far doorway. This time I stuck my hands out before me and stepped forward. I kept walking, keeping my hands along the walls, not trusting my senses. There was no sign of him.

"Hyginos?" I called. Great. Maybe he really did mean to kill me. I walked along for a while, following the wall, until suddenly my hand struck a gap. I turned and saw -

The same window I had started at. Was it? Yes, there was the rope ladder right there, and the frescoes at the bottom of the tower of ships and fish. Definitely the same window. I looked to my left, and saw the same passage extending forward, just as it seemed to be going before me and behind me: mirrored in all directions. "Hyginos," I said. "At no point did I ever say this was funny!"

I threw out my hand and rammed the tilted mirror to the left of me in anger. It turned, and I saw a stone wall behind it. I struck it again. It began to spin, quickly, and I caught it with my hand at the half-measure to make an opening. I stepped into a small alcove. There was a small, perfectly spherical impression in the wall. In the center of this sphere there was a tiny hole, too small for me to look through, but I could see light coming through it.

Realization began to dawn. This was a Camera Obscura. And for a camera obscura to work it needed two things: a surface to project onto, and a dark room. I turned the mirror and shut myself into the alcove, which became pitch black for a second. But then, almost instantly, the pupil of the camera did its work, and the alcove filled with the light of the room beyond. I found myself staring into the reflection of a small library filled with scrolls, which looked similar to the first room I had been in with the stairs. At least, there was one stalagmite column with a corinthian capital rising from the floor, and upon it was a single papyrus scroll.

Next to the books was a furnace, which appeared to have hot coals inside. I could see Hyginos standing there, and he was holding a sword. On the ground was a giant Egg made of bronze. Hyginos was reciting a spell. It was one of the spells from the scroll Sophistic Solon had just sent us, invoking the name of Agathodaimon to bind the daimon of a man to his will.

With horror I realized that Hyginos was attempting to bind *my* soul to his will. I could feel it, as though my soul were a bird, fluttering in my chest. And his words were reaching through the wall at my back, the wall between us, grabbing me like a giant vice, while I was stuck staring at the projection of the camera on the back of the mirror. I tried to push my way out of the alcove but I found the mirror was stuck. Trapped. I was going to be bound in the midst of the magician's labyrinth, and made into his slave.

He took the sword and swung it in a great arc, striking the Egg with it. I saw it explode in a torrent of Fire, Pumice and Ash. A burst of flames filled the room. Hyginos was nowhere to be seen. I felt his spell closing over my soul, and I was losing my will. Already my head was filled with strange thoughts - almost adoration - for a person whom I had felt I despised just this morning —

Then, something happened which I did not expect. Out of the torrent of fire I saw a single bird appear: the Benu bird of Thoth, the phoenix. And at once, like a royal decree swiftly meting justice, I felt every gateway of Hyginos' spells break in my mind, a series of proclamations rendered mute. I do not know if Hyginos saw the God. To this day, I think he was only for me. But Hyginos knew that his spell had failed.

Yet when the flames cleared I could not see him, and I was still stuck in that small alcove.

I struggled to get out for a time, trying every means I could to get the door open. I pried at the panel at the back of the mirror. I pounded. It never seemed to budge, as if it had been wedged shut. The air grew musty and hot, and I shoved my nose against the small opening in the camera. Time began to stretch. I grew hungry, and then strange dreams began to enter my head.

I dreamed I was walking down the same endless hallway from before, from behind the mirror. I was trying to find Hyginos, to demand that he would let me out. Then I thought I saw him coming towards me, but as I got closer, I saw that it was the troglodyte. The grey folds of his skin were swaying as he walked, and, expressionless, he had an object in his hands that he was meant to give to me, something that I was supposed to have —

I woke up suddenly. It was night, and I could see the Moon right in front of me. It was shining through a perfectly round window on the other side of the library, and being reflected through the camera obscura. Then I saw the shadow of Hyginos moving through the projection, with a small candle in front of him, lighting up his face. He was creeping up inside and outside the field of the projection, and then he was right next to the slit. I could hear him breathing.

"Hyginos," I said. "Will you let me out."

He ignored this. "You know," he said, "afterwards, my father always said I imagined it. But I swear when I visited that labyrinth in Crocodilopolis they had slaves — Jews, of course, Egyptians always enslave Jews — " he must have been baiting me, "and these slaves were turning giant gears that moved the chambers of the labyrinth around. Such that, no two journeys in the labyrinth would be the same. And the Egyptian masters whipped these slaves, they whipped them! Some of them even died." He smacked his lips. "But the labyrinth was always shifting, always changing. Even if you walked back into the same room, its characteristics would have changed."

"Why were you putting a spell on me? To bend my mind to your will?"

"I told you. I like you."

"This does not seem like a nice way to treat your friends."

"Psa," said Hyginos. "You are the only Egyptian I like."

"This was never about the curse was it?"

"Maybe," said Hyginos. "It might have been about the curse. Do you know anything about this magic?"

I swallowed. "Not particularly," I gasped.

"That's true you really don't seem to know much about magic, do you? Otherwise you would have seen through these illusions. Still, you are cute."

"Hyginos," I said. "If that is what you are implying I am not interested in being your lover. That is not a practice which thrills me."

"No?" said Hyginos. "And what if the only way I let you out was if you...?"

"Obviously I would rather die here," I said with more bravery than I felt.

"Then I would let you die."

"What would you tell them at the Musaion, when I disappeared?"

"That you had refused to identify the markings on my door and then fled. That you can never trust an Egyptian and you should never have been admitted to the academy in the first place."

I was silent. They would believe that, and also, it was close to the truth.

"How about this," said Hyginos. "We'll play a game. I'm going to let you out now, and set you free in the laby- rinth. If I catch you, you will have to do whatever I want you to before you can go free. But if you find your way out, you can go your way. Either way we will never speak of this again. Otherwise, I'm being sincere, I actually am content to let you rot in there."

I thought of Hyginos, the strange pervert who lived alone in his bizarre labyrinth, lighting cats on fire and deliberately insulting peoples' religions, and I believed him.

"Alright," I said. "Deal."

There was a scraping sound. He seemed to pull a lever. Then I heard gears grinding, just like in his fantasy of the labyrinth of Ammenemes, and the wall behind me in the alcove began to turn. It spun all the way around, and then I was in the room with the library and the furnace.

Hyginos was not there, of course, which only made me more nervous. He could be anywhere. He meant to play with me. The floor of the room was covered in soot from the furnace and the explosion from before. The scroll-racks of the library were still there, and somehow the book on the stalagmite capital was miraculously untouched. I went over to the round window beyond, thinking that it might be the same one I had glimpsed the troglodyte in on that night long ago, and that maybe I could climb out. I glanced out - and found myself looking down a thousand foot drop of sheer cliff to the sea. It was calm, and there was no city in sight. The night sky was blue.

How? We were far from the harbor. It was all an illusion. But maybe, like the mirror in the cavern, it covered some still worse fate - a pit full of spikes, or some other trap. There was no way to know whether if I jumped through the window, I would actually be outside. I turned away from the window, and saw another door in the far wall. I went forward and opened it, thinking all the time that Hyginos had meant for me to come this way.

I found myself on top of a causeway running along the side of a canal. The water in the canal was as black as ink, and seemed to be very deep. On the other side there were grates near the ceiling, through which I could see the familiar street outside - the same abandoned building where Osarseph and I had crouched and had one of our arguments about Moses. It was tantalizing. I knew I was close, but the water was diaphanous and black, as if it were made of shadow, and I was scared - I did not want to brave it. Hyginos would have intended this too. I had to do something to throw off his expectations, but what?

At that moment, standing on the strange causeway in that infinite house, I thought of all my possible paths through the unknown labyrinth. In my mind's eye, I saw myself being pursued by Hyginos, who had a diabolical means to create illusions and some unknown mechanism to move walls. Every way I could take he would anticipate. He had the entire advantage, I was entirely disadvantaged. I knew nothing of the labyrinth.

Except, the one thing I could control was my intention. He was assuming that I would be doing everything I could to try to get out: jumping out windows, even swimming across canals to pry open tiny grates in the ceiling. But what he would not expect would be for me to attempt to go further *into* the labyrinth, and find the mysterious troglodyte he had hidden inside. And if I reached this troglodyte - who I was sure was real, and that I had not imagined him - perhaps I could have a hostage to buy my freedom from him. Assuming the troglodyte was not just some pet he had kept for one of his games. I decided then to search for the center of the labyrinth, rather than trying to get out.

So I walked down the causeway, feeling along the wall with my hands. I had gone about five meters before my hand went through a wall, finally catching one of Hyginos' illusions. I looked left and right, half expecting him to jump out at me, and then pushed through.

I stepped into a room that was the opposite of a pyramid.

I was looking down into a pit, with a series of square terraces leading into the center. It was like a step pyramid, but the steps led down. At the bottom there was a well. Water was pouring into the well from one of the sides of the pit, tumbling down in a series of waterfalls, coming from a grate in the wall. It was connected to the canal: the water was the same inky-black color. Dimly, in the half light, I could make out a small ladder set into the side of the well down which the water was pouring.

I scrambled down the steps of the pyramid, grabbing myself by the knees to keep myself from tumbling down. At the bottom layer I found myself standing in a thin film of water from the flood, perfectly black like the night sky. And then, suddenly, it was the night sky. The black water was reflecting the sky, like a mirror. It was filled with stars.

I looked up, and saw the zodiac and the empyrean above me. There was Venus, the evening star. There was Orion, and Leo, and the Seven Sisters. I could see the forms of the decans glittering down at me, and they were smiling. They seemed to speak to me. The cosmos was ascending above my head, like a crown, going higher and higher and ascending layers.

By whatever art Hyginos had made this place, it was beautiful. Then I heard his small hiccoughing laughter from somewhere beyond. Without any way of knowing whether he had intended me to take this route, I pulled myself into the well, and clambered down the ladder. I went down a long time, or seemed to.

The well exited into a chamber made of bronze. There were two torches guarding a door made of orichalcum and inlaid with gold. I opened it, and found myself on a stairway in the sky. Now, although I had traveled down, I was above the decans, looking upon the same forms of the zodiac that before I had been looking up at. They smiled up at me. Before me was an endless flight of golden stairs which seemed to lead up. They were translucent, and made more of thought than of matter. I began climbing up, into the sky.

The heavens began to change from black to blue, and

the stars beneath me began to vanish. Then it became purple, and as my ascent continued, it shifted to pink. I realized, gradually, that somewhere the Sun was rising, and this was a mirror to capture it. The light was growing and increasing in strength, getting brighter and brighter, and at any moment I thought I must see the disk of the Sun come spinning beneath me, blinding me, when I came to a door in a wall at the top of the stairs. I opened it, and stepped through into the first room I had come to in the labyrinth, the room with the stalagmite and stalactite pillars, and the two sets of stairs, although now I was on the ceiling and not on the floor. I could tell this because I could see the door through which I had entered from before.

I walked down the stairs which curved from the ceiling to the floor, although now they did not seem so impossible as before. Then, forgetting my earlier resolution, I decided to see if I could get out of the labyrinth the way I came in. I walked down the same hallway that was black, ochre and pink that I had entered from before. There was the statue of Athena, and the front door. I opened it.

There was a room before me, filled with stone couches covered with an abundance of cushions. In the far wall was a perfectly round window, covered with a wooden shutter, with a brass handle in the center. In the room was a table, and a small chair. And there in the chair was the troglodyte, sleeping. I had found what I had originally intended, but not the way out.

I walked around the room, careful not to wake the creature. Around me I could feel the familiar tension I associated with dawn about to break. I stood before it, and watched it sleep. Its white, wispy eyebrows seemed to embrace its forehead, which tapered to an almost conical skull. His skin was off-grey, and his flesh was mottled and ancient. Folds of skin hung from his hands and legs, like a giant bat. His skin was weathered and wrinkled, from what looked to be centuries of living in caves.

But he seemed to be well cared-for, and healthy. Interesting. As I could feel the morning about to begin, I weighed my options, and for some reason - some ghost was nudging me - I decided to play my card, or my good fortune.

I threw open the round window, sending the sunlight blindingly into the room, waking the troglodyte at once.

"Hyginos!" I shouted. "I am here with your creature! Come find me!"

I heard from somewhere far off the sound of scraping. I waited. The troglodyte was blinking in the Sun, and its strange, deep eyes seemed to be regarding me with some interest. Then I heard feet padding down the hall, and Hyginos came to the room.

"You've given up?" he said. "You want to end the game so easily?"

"No," I said. "Why do you have this creature here?"

"It is of no interest to me," said Hyginos. "It amuses me. I keep it as a past-time. Now, seeing as you have forfeited your side of the bet..."

"I don't believe you," I said. "You care for this creature in an uncommon way."

"Well perhaps I am over-fond of him. You, on the other hand, have lost, so - "

I positioned myself next to the window, so the troglodyte was between me and him. I could see the street outside.

"What if," I said, "after I *service* you," being sure to spit the word, "I were to tell people at the Musaion about this troglodyte you have here?"

Yes, I saw it in his eyes, alarm. "Don't do that. Then I will say what I said before, that you are an untrustworthy Egyptian."

"Yes, but then I will be at the Musaion, doing my work, and therefore trustworthy. I will not have mysteriously vanished in the night. And I will tell them that you blackmailed me."

"Why should they believe you?"

"Because this is a ridiculous situation anyways. And since the plague began at your house, I have reason to call the magistrate and tell them to investigate this residence you have here. What is this troglodyte to you?"

"Nothing," he said.

"I don't believe you. I don't think you built this labyrinth to trap people, to keep people in, or even to satisfy your childhood love of illusions of Crocodilopolis. You did not build this to keep people in, but to keep them out. You are trying to protect this troglodyte."

"Ridiculous," said Hyginos. "He is nothing to me, nothing but a pet."

"Really?" I said. "Then what if I throttled him right now?"

"No!" shouted Hyginos, stepping forward with passion. "Don't do that! I mean, he is dear to me, and why do you come through here violating the inhabitants of my house?"

"So this cave-dweller is important to you then. Not just as an amusement. And you are upset with me for even suggesting I mention him to some of our fellow scholars."

"Do I pry into your business?" said Hyginos.

"Do I trap you in my labyrinth?"

"Step away from him," Hyginos commanded.

"No," I said, grabbing the troglodyte by the neck and pulling him up next to me. "Let me go, or I will break his neck." The troglodyte began to wail, like it was crying.

"Gods damn you!" Hyginos shrieked. "Do I manhandle your family?"

I stopped, and almost released my grip. "Family?" I said. "This troglodyte is your *family*?"

"He's my grandfather you Egyptian bastard. If you kill him I'll kill you."

"What?" I said, trying to take this in. "You're calling *me* a bastard? So you are not well-bred after all. That is why you like to insult others."

"Let him go," Hyginos said.

"Let me out," I said.

"Never. I'll kill you for touching him and insulting my blood."

"Yet I have your kin for a shield." I threw the ancient troglodyte towards him, and Hyginos caught him. He dissolved into whimpers, clutching the old man to his breast. I watched the two of them, fascinated. Hyginos descended from a troglodyte.

He stared up at me, glaring. "I am never letting you out of here alive," he said.

"Okay," I said. And I jumped out the window.

I sprained my ankle in the fall, and wandered back to the Musaion in a daze, unsure how I would tell Sumethres and the others about the strange and terrific things I had just seen.

I settled on not mentioning it to anyone, ever, which as you will see was the wrong decision.

Back at the Musaion, I tried to pretend it was life as normal. That afternoon, Eratosthenes and Archimedes summoned me.

"How was it, by the way," said Eratosthenes, "at Hyginos house? Did you notice any black magic?"

"No," I said, "no, definitely not."

"In my day," said Archimedes, "scholars of the Musaion did not even mention such things. Now Psa, did you get a chance to read my book? Do you have it with you?"

I shifted uncomfortably. I had in fact given it to Sophistic Solon. Eratosthenes seemed to pick up on this, which surprised me — and then I remembered that the only reason I had reached the Library of the Ulterior in the first place was technically because I was in the employ of its antagonist, of the person who most wanted to wipe the *other* Library out of existence.

"No," I said. "I don't, sir, my apologies."

"But you did have a chance to read it, yes?"

"I was interested sir, but I am not sure I fully understood."

"But you understood the general concept."

"You are making a model of the heavens."

"And that is why," Archimedes said, sitting down next to a table, "I wanted to speak with you one last time."

"About what we spoke of before?"

"I need to know about the secrets of Heliopolis."

I sighed. "I told you, sir, as far as I know there *are* no secrets of Heliopolis, but I am not initiated."

"But what of this teaching of a central fire? Of Philolaos, and that the Earth goes around it?" He gestured to Eratosthenes. "Where is Aristarchus, anyway?"

"Away," said Eratosthenes. "Visiting family."

"I do not know about a central fire," I said. "Our teachings concerning the Sun is that he revolves through the land of the dead, and that in the underworld confronts the demons who wish to pervert our world and thereby maintains cosmic order. We are chiefly concerned with

133

maintaining the incantations to ensure that he continues to cross the sky."

"Ah," said Archimedes, "I see."

"In that sense," I continued, "What does it matter if the Earth goes around the Sun, or the Sun goes around the Earth? We are only concerned that we are in harmony with him, sir, and that the order of our society is good. But we know of course," I could not resist throwing in this, "all of these things you speak of, have known them eternally, and will know them again at the end of time."

"It is true then, what they say," said Archimedes. "You Egyptians have two religions."

At this moment there was a commotion outside the door.

"I will come in!" shouted a voice. Hyginos. A sinking feeling entered my gut. Great, what did he want?

He burst in through some of the attendants and marched into the hall. "Hyginos," said Eratosthenes, "What brings you here?"

"This man," he said pointing at me, "Is a liar and a sorcerer!"

"What?" said Archimedes, "What is the meaning of this?"

"Oh Lords," said Hyginos, "It is true what the oracle said. 'Justice will be served by the next of kin.' When I brought this man to my house to dispel the bad influences he met my grandfather; my grandfather recognized him, sirs, having seen him out the window on the day my door-step was cursed!"

Ah. Troglodytes could talk then.

"Really?" said Eratosthenes, "I find this highly unlikely. Is he sure it was not just another Egyptian?"

"Quite sure," said Hyginos. "In fact — he is absolutely positive!"

"Psammetichus," said Eratosthenes. "Is this true?"

"No, my Lords," I said. "Absolutely not."

They put me in one of Eratosthene's private cells and barred the door, and went to fetch the magistrate. I had maintained my innocence, but, in the presence of such testimony and with so much property having been lost, is it any wonder no one wanted to believe me?

So I was under house arrest and awaiting my fate. It was not an unpleasant room. It was on the third floor, and it faced the harbor and the view of the city, extending over the Greek quarter, with the Lighthouse beyond. I could see smoke rising from the Serapaeum, and I knew someone had just made an offering. The sunlight was catching the tomb of Alexander, whose crystal cupola refracted it into many colors.

The Sun. I thought of my conversation with Archimedes, looked towards the sun, and began to pray.

Oh Thoth, who writes the ledger of Eternity, avert for

me this bad thing, as one who loves justice. You who, allied with Moon, keeps the Sun in its course. I have not spoken against the innocent; I have loved wisdom, I have loved honor; in the holy name of Ta-tanen, I pray.

At that moment someone unbarred the door, and I thought for a wild instant that my prayer had been answered, but then I saw that it was just Eratosthenes' manservant: a small, withered old man, come in to offer me bread and water. The Head Librarian was not uncivilized, and even as a suspect I was still a guest.

The servant looked familiar even though I had never seen him before. There was something about his movements that I recognized, although I could not put my finger on it, not by the light of day...

"Ah!" I said. "It's you! You're Sophistic Solon."

The old man did not say anything to me, nor did he meet my eyes. He set down a tray with three loaves and a cup in front of me.

There were so many things I wanted to ask him — why, if he was in Eratosthenes employ he had taken it upon himself to construct a new library catalog, or perhaps for some strange reason they were in on it together? Or where had his prodigious knowledge come from, that he knew so much of things forbidden, things forgotten, if he was just an old servant?

But I did not have much time before he went out the door, so instead I said to him: "Please, if it is you, you must help me. They will execute or imprison me for sure. Please, will you find my friend Sumethres? He can help. He can get me out."

The old man did not say anything to me, but walked out the door and bolted it again, without ever acknowledging he had heard me.

They brought me before the King. "Bow before the incarnation of Harpocrates, the keeper of secrets!" a herald proclaimed.

"Yes, yes, let's just get through the Egypto-nonsense," I muttered. I bowed in the traditional way, not that anyone attending would understand.

King Ptolemy III was sitting on a throne made of electrum, woven in the design of vines and ivy. The crier was sitting at his feet, and the magistrate with three judges were off to his left. A tribunal. Not as intimidating as the Tribunal of the Dead, but in this instance it seemed it might lead to the same result.

"Bring forth the accuser," cried the magistrate.

Hyginos stepped out from the shadows of one of the forecourts. "Oh King," he said. "I stand before you a wronged man."

"In what sense are you wronged?" said King Ptolemy.

"This man," Hyginos gestured towards me, all theater, as usual, "has poisoned my cows."

"Indeed," said the magistrate, "that is the accusation, and need I remind you oh King, that this has caused a plague, a curse to fall upon half the livestock of the city of Alexandria."

"Is it true then," said the King, gesturing to me, "that you can prove that this man, has caused *this* destruction of property, which seems to come from the will of the Gods?"

"It is," cried Hyginos, and then the court turned to me.

"And how do you plead?" said the magistrate.

I had made up my mind while I waited in the cell. "Guilty! Incredibly guilty, sirs."

Silence fell. The whole court stopped and stared. Hyginos' mouth was agape as he looked at me.

"Do you really mean," said the King, "to imply that you have caused such pestilence through the course of a single magical action? That you yourself would have this power? And why would you do it?"

"I did it," I said, "because Hyginos has made a mockery of my people, and I hate the Greeks, sir." If you're going to get sentenced to death, no half measures.

There were no gasps. The silence grew deeper and more intense.

"Indeed: I loathe your people, you foul conquerors

who lack culture, and pervert our sacred rites. Hyginos lit a cat on fire, and I was disgusted at the insult to my sacred Goddess. For too long have you Greeks occupied our land, this land that is sacred to the Gods, and used it to satisfy your base instincts. Yet look, is not the Nile Delta sacred? Do not the Gods descend from their course in the sky to speak to us? Do not even the movements of the planets show that this is the center of the world?

"I stand before the tribunal unrepentant, ready to be devoured, for it takes justice to meet justice, and if you lack justice, there is no justice. Therefore, lords, visit what sentence you command upon me: my soul will not recognize it, and I will go to the abyss in disdain of you and your foul abuse of authority. I have not sinned against the Gods."

Absolute silence. Hyginos had his hand over his mouth.

"Never before," said King Ptolemy, "have I heard such *insolence* come from the mouths of one of you barbarians!"

"Quite eloquent, though," commented the magistrate.

The King ignored this. "There is no sentence sufficient for you, *you* who stand before a *God* and speak with such disdain. Not if we fed your liver to all the crows scattered to the four corners of the world could there be such a punishment!"

I almost shat myself. "Lord," I shouted confidently.

"Take me to Ammit: take me to Hell." A boot shoved me down onto the ground.

"Draw and quarter him in the Agora," said the King. "Make a proclamation so all citizens can see. Then cut out his heart and sacrifice it in the Serapaeum — perhaps this will please the Gods and end his curse. At dawn tomorrow."

"One thing is for sure," said the magistrate as I was taken away, "there is never going to be another Egyptian we let attend the Musaion."

I was in a cell under the Royal Palace awaiting my execution when the ghost returned to me.

"Well, I'm about to die," I said. "I'll be with you shortly."

The ghost pointed its thumb inwards, to its mouth insistently.

"Ah. You want me to write your story."

The ghost nodded in assent.

"While there is still time. Before I die. Of course."

I called to the guard, and asked for papyrus and a pen.

"So," he said, "You want to write your last will and request?"

"Please," I said. "Can you fetch it for me?"

"You expect hospitality, barbarian, you who were so insulting to our King? Yet you do not even have manners," he said.

So I begged. I could feel the akh of the God behind me. And I feared the Heavenly Tribunal far more than I feared Ptolemy III.

The guard relented and brought me pen, papyrus and ink. I sat down, and although I was more terrified than I had ever been in my life, I began to write:

THE ARETALOGY OF IMHOUTHES

Nectanebus on hearing this, being extremely vexed with the deserters from the temple and wishing to ascertain their number speedily by a list, ordered Nechautis, who then performed the duties of archidicastes, to investigate the book within a month, if possible. Nechautis conducted his researches with much strenuousness, and brought the list to the King after spending only two days instead of thirty upon the inquiry. On reading the book the King was quite amazed at the divine power in the story, and finding that there were twenty-six priests who conducted the god from Heliopolis to Memphis, he assigned to each of their descendants the due post of prophet. Not content with this, after completing the renewal of the book, he enriched Asclepius himself with three hundred and thirty arurae more of corn-land, especially because he had heard through the book that the God had been worshiped with marks of great reverence by Mencheres.

144

Having often begun the translation of the said book in the Greek tongue, I learnt at length how to proclaim it, but while I was in the full tide of composition my ardor was restrained by the greatness of the story, because I was about to make it public; for to gods alone, not to mortals, is it permitted to describe the mighty deeds of the gods. For if I failed, not only was I ashamed before men, but also hindered by the reproaches that I should incur if the God were vexed, and by the poverty of my description, in course of completion, of his undying virtue. But if I did the God a service, both my life would be happy and my fame undying; for the God is disposed to confer benefits, since even those whose pious ardor is only for the moment are repeatedly preserved by him after the healing art has failed against diseases which have overtaken them. Therefore avoiding rashness I was waiting for the favorable occasion afforded by old age, and putting off the fulfillment of my promise; for then especially is youth wont to aim too high, since immaturity and enterprise too quickly extend our zeal. But when a period of three years had elapsed, in which I was no longer working, and for three years my mother was distracted by an ungodly quartan ague which had seized her, at length having with difficulty comprehended we came as suppliants before the god, entreating him to grant my mother recovery from the disease. He, having shown himself favorable, as he is to all, in dreams, cured her by simple remedies; and we rendered due thanks to our preserver by sacrifices. When I too afterwards was suddenly seized with a pain in my right side, I quickly hastened to the helper of the human race, and he, being again disposed to pity, listened to me, and displayed still more effectively his peculiar clemency, which, as I am intending to recount his terrible powers, I will substantiate.

It was night, when every living creature was asleep except those in pain, but divinity showed itself the more effectively; a violent fever burned me, and I was convulsed with loss of breath and coughing, owing to the pain proceeding from my side. Heavy in the head with my troubles I was lapsing half-conscious into sleep, and my mother, as a mother would for her child (and she is by nature affectionate), being extremely grieved at my agonies was sitting without enjoying even a short period of slumber, when suddenly she perceived — it was no dream or sleep, for her eyes were open immovably, though not seeing clearly, for a divine and terrifying vision came to her, easily preventing her from observing the god himself or his servants, whichever it was. In any case there was someone whose height was more than human, clothed in shining raiment and carrying in his left hand a book, who after merely regarding me two or three times from head to foot disappeared. When she had recovered herself, she tried, still trembling, to wake me, and finding that the fever had left me and that much sweat was pouring off me, did reverence to the manifestation of the god, and then wiped me and made me more collected. When I spoke with her, she wished to declare the virtue of the god, but I, anticipating her, told her all myself; for everything that she saw in the vision appeared to me in dreams.

After these pains in my side had ceased and the god had given me yet another assuaging cure, I proclaimed his benefits. But when we had again besought his favors by sacrifices to the best of our ability, he demanded through the priest who serves him in the ceremonies the fulfillment of the promise long ago announced to him, and we, although knowing ourselves to be debtors in neither sacrifices nor votive offering, nevertheless supplicated him again with them. But when he said repeatedly that he cared not for these but for what had been previously promised, I was at a loss, and with difficulty, since I disparaged it, felt the divine obligation of the composition.

But since thou hadst once noticed, master, that I was neglecting the divine book, invoking thy providence and filled with thy divinity I hastened to the inspired task of the history. And I hope to extend by my proclamation the fame of thy inventive-

147

ness; for I unfolded truly by a physical treatise in another book the convincing account of the creation of the world. Throughout the composition I have filled up defects and struck out superfluities, and in telling a rather long tale I have spoken briefly and narrated once for all a complicated story.

Hence, master, I conjecture that the book has been completed in accordance with thy favor, not with my aim; for such a record in writing suits thy divinity. And as the discoverer of this art, Asclepius, greatest of gods and my teacher, thou art distinguished by the thanks of all men. For every gift of a votive offering or sacrifice lasts only for the immediate moment, and presently perishes, while a written record is an undying meed of gratitude, from time to time renewing its youth in the memory. Every Greek tongue will tell thy story, and every Greek man will worship the son of Ptah, Imouthes. Assemble hither, ye kindly and good men; avaunt ye malignant and impious! Assemble, all ye, who by serving the god have been cured of diseases, ye who practice the healing art, ye who will labor as zealous followers of virtue, ye who have been blessed by great abundance of benefits, ye who have been saved from the dangers of the sea! For every place has been penetrated by the saving power of the God.

I now purpose to recount his miraculous manifestations, the greatness of his power, the gifts of his benefits. The history is this: King Mencheres by displaying his piety in the obsequies of three gods, and being successful in winning fame through the book, has won eternal glory. He presented to the tombs of Asclepius son of Hephaestus, Horus son of Hermes, and also Caleoibis son of Apollo money in abundance, and received as recompense his fill of prosperity. For Egypt was then free from war for this reason, and flourished with abundant crops, since subject countries prosper by the piety of their ruler, and on the other hand owing to his impiety they are consumed by evils. The manner in which the god Asclepius bade Mencheres busy himself with his tomb...

At this moment I stopped, because I heard tapping on the bars of my window. I looked up and in the moonlight saw the face of Sumethres staring down at me.

"Sumet," I whispered.

"Yes," he said. "And I've brought a friend."

Osarseph stuck his face into the window and held up a file. "We're getting you out, man."

"Are you crazy?" I said. "The guards will see, and you'll get killed."

"One of your scholastic friends is distracting them," said Sumet.

"Who?" I asked.

"I don't know, old guy." Osarseph started work filing

away one of the iron bars. Was it Sophistic Solon?

"Do you have any things?" said Sumet.

"Just this," I said, holding up my unfinished book.

"What's that?"

"The Book of Thoth," I said.

Sumet shook his head. "You're crazy. You're turning into a Greek."

"I need to go back to the Library."

"No way," said Sumet. "You'll get seen."

"Just once," I said.

"Buddy," said Sumet. "What you need is to *get out of Alexandria.*"

It was Eratosthenes who had distracted the guards, but I never found out why. I had no chance to ask. Under cover of darkness, Sumet and Osarseph got me back to my cell, where I gathered my personal effects. Then, ignoring their protests, I went and visited Sophistic Solon one last time.

I went up to the upper gallery on the right hand side of the main atrium, where Solon had first shown me the book, the section on property records. I took my *Aretalogy* and shoved it into the recession where in the Ulterior had been the Book, as far back as it would go.

Then, having planted my book within the Library of Alexandria, I left the city before first light, catching a boat to the South. I never returned.

PART TWO

Hermopolis

But there is also the other form of time. This is the circle, which neither begins or ends, but, like the waters of the River Hapi, continues its cycles of inundation. I would never return to Alexandria, not while a ban lay on my head. The Library of the Ulterior would always remain a mystery to me.

However — there are other Libraries. Other forms of memory and forgetfulness. And this is the world I was meant to discover.

The barque cut the waters of the River, as golden light filtered down from the West. The water around the boat was brown. In the distance, mirroring the sky, it appeared blue. Pike and small fishes were milling about. There was a boatman I had hired in Memphis who was guiding the barge, pushing a pole against the shallows and propelling it forward. We were going South, South of the Faiyum, South of anywhere too Greek.

"You have come a long way," the boatman commented.

"Yes sir," I replied. He was older than me. We did not say anything for a long time.

"Are you going on a pilgrimage to Abydos?"

"No," I said. "Not for me. Not yet at any rate."

"You are a scribe," he said. It was not a question.

"Yes," I said.

"That is wonderful," he said. "Maybe you can write

my will."

"Maybe," I said.

"If you do that," he said. "I will not charge you for this journey, for I can only take you to Khemenu anyway. But you are going on."

"I am not sure where I am going," I said.

"It seems to me," he said, "That you have spent a lot of time among the Greeks. Is that right?"

"Yes sir," I said. "I did not know what was good for me."

"But now you are coming back to the land of the real Egypt. This is good. You got out of there."

"Yes," I said.

"Hmm," said the boatman. He was silent for a long time. We pushed through the marshes, passing by fields and date palms, shallows where the ibis preened and some-times we saw children playing. I saw a vulture flying over-head, watching over all.

"It seems to me," said the boatman, "that you have come South for a reason. You are searching for something."

I was silent.

"You are looking for the Book of Thoth."

What again? From my own countrymen? I smiled. People who could not read had all these notions. "Sir," I said. "There is no one Book of Thoth, there are many —"

"Oh," he said. "So you do not know the story."

"What story?"

"The story of Setne Khamwas and Naneferkaptah," said the boatman. "Let's see..."

"Once there was a Prince named Setne Khamwas, the son of Ramses II. He was a high priest of Ptah at Memphis, and a very learned scribe and magician. He spent his time in the study of ancient monuments and books. He it was who first set about restoring the ancient monuments of Egypt, thousands of years after they had been built. But above all other things he desired knowledge.

"One day, he heard of the existence of a book of magic written by the god Thoth himself. It was kept in the tomb of a prince named Naneferkaptah, buried in the City of the Dead outside Memphis. He had lived long ago, in the distant past, in the time of the Pyramids. So Prince Khamwas went with his brother Inaros to the necropolis, and after a long search they found this man's tomb.

"They pried open the door, ignoring the curses meant to bewitch intruders. They passed by the false doors: they were not confused. They came into the tomb, and they saw the magic book sitting there, radiating a strong light. Prince Khamwas went up to take this book, but as he reached out his hand, two spirits came out of it and accosted him, howling.

"It was the spirits of Naneferkaptah, and his wife Ahwere, and with her was a child.

"'Oh Prince Khamwas,' said Ahwere, 'You think that you want this knowledge of Thoth, that you want to know magic. But my husband and I paid for it dearly. Long ago, the two of us were the only children of the King Merneptah —'

"Hang on a second," I said. "Was not the real Khamwaset rightly the brother of Merneptah? In which case these two siblings, who are also husband and wife, would be his niece and nephew? Historically, that is?"

"What's History?" said the boatman. "Who's telling this story - me, or you? And do you want to hear about the Book of Thoth, or not?"

"'Oh Prince Khamwas,' said Ahwere, 'We loved each other very much and wanted to marry. But our father, King Merneptah, would not let us. He wanted to marry his son to the daughter of a general, and his daughter to the son of a general.'

"'So I went,' she said, 'To the chief steward, to beg him to plead with the King on my behalf. He did, and he begged the King to allow his two children to marry. And when he asked him this, he became very distressed. In fact:

he fell silent.'

"So the steward asked, 'Why, oh King, are you so distressed? Is something wrong?'

"'It is you who distresses me. If it so happens that I have only two children, is it right to marry the one to the other? I will marry Naneferkaptah to the daughter of a general, and I will marry Ahwere to the son of another general, so that our family may increase!'

"'When the time came for the banquet to be set before the King, they came for me and took me to the banquet. But my heart was very sad and I did not have my former looks. The King said to me: 'Ahwere was it you who sent to me with those foolish words, "Let me marry Naneferkaptah, my elder brother?"

"'I said to him: "Let me marry the son of a general, and let him marry the daughter of another general, so that our family may increase!" I laughed and the King laughed.

"But it seemed this had caused the King to change his mind. When the steward of the palace came the King said to him: 'Steward, let Ahwere be taken to the house of Naneferkaptah tonight, and let all sorts of beautiful things be taken with her.'

"I was taken as a wife to the house of Naneferkaptah that night, and the King sent me a present of silver and gold, and all the royal household sent me presents. Naneferkaptah made holiday with me and he entertained the whole royal household. He slept with me that night and found me pleasing. He slept with me again and again, and we loved each other.

"When my time of purification came I made no more purification. It was reported to the King, and his heart was very happy. The King had many things taken out of the treasury and sent me presents of silver, gold, and royal linen, all very beautiful. When my time of bearing came, I bore this boy who is before you, who was named Merib. He was entered in the register of the House of Life.

"It so happened that my brother Naneferkaptah had no occupation on earth but walking on the desert of Memphis, reading the writings that were in the tombs of the Kings and on the stelae of the scribes of the House of Life and the writings that were on the other monuments, for his zeal concerning writings was very great.

"After this there was a procession in honor of Ptah, and Naneferkaptah went into the temple to worship. As he was walking behind the procession, reading the writings on the shrines of the gods, an old priest saw him and laughed. Naneferkaptah said to him: 'Why are you laughing at me?' He said: 'I am not laughing at you. I am laughing because you are reading writings that have no importance for anyone. If you desire to read writings, come to me and I will have you taken to the place where that book is that Thoth wrote with his own hand, when he came down following the other gods. Two spells are written in it. When you recite the first spell you will charm the sky, the earth, the netherworld, the mountains, and the waters. You will discover what all the birds of the sky and all the reptiles are saying. You will see the fish of the deep, though there are twenty-one divine cubits of water over them. When you recite the second spell, it will happen that, whether you are in the netherworld or in your form on earth, you will see Re appearing in the sky with his Ennead, and the Moon in its form of rising.'

"Naneferkaptah said to him: 'As the King lives, tell me a good thing that you desire, so that I may do it for you, and you send me to the place where this book is!'

"The priest said to Naneferkaptah: 'If you wish to be sent to the place where this book is you must give me a hundred pieces of silver for my burial, and you must endow me with two priestly stipends tax-free.'

"Naneferkaptah called a servant and had the hundred pieces of silver given to the priest. He added the two stipends and had the priest endowed with them tax-free.

"The priest said to Naneferkaptah: 'The book in question is in the middle of the water of Coptos in a box of iron. In the box of iron is a box of copper. In the box of copper is a box of juniper wood. In the box of juniper wood is a box of ivory and ebony. In the box of ivory and ebony is a box of silver. In the box of silver is a box of gold, and in it is the book. There are six miles of serpents, scorpions, and all kinds of reptiles around the box in which the book is, and there is an eternal serpent, the World Serpent, around this same box.'"

"Wait," I said. "The Book is in the Nile?"

"In this very water we are over now," said the boat-man. "Although you must remember, it is at Coptos."

"Have you been to Coptos?"

"No," said the boatman. "I have never been that far South."

"So you have not seen this book for yourself."

"You are not paying attention," said the boatman. "There are six miles of scorpions, serpents, and all kinds of reptiles surrounding the six boxes within which is the for-bidden book, and unlike you I have not gotten the bug for knowledge. Why would I waste my time? That is a lot of scorpions to get through."

"When the priest had thus spoken to Naneferkaptah, he did not know where on earth he was. He came out of the temple, he told me everything that had happened to him.

"He said to me: 'I will go to Coptos, I will bring this book, hastening back to the north again.'

"But I chided the priest, saying: 'May Neith curse you for having told him these dreadful things! You have brought me combat, you have brought me strife. The region of Thebes, I now find it abhorrent.' I did what I could with Naneferkaptah to prevent him from going to Coptos; he did not listen to me. He went to the King and told him every-thing that the priest had said to him.

"The King said to him: 'What is it that you want?'

"Naneferkaptah said to him: 'Let the ship of the King be given to me with its equipment. I will take Ahwere and her boy Merib to the south with me, I will bring this book without delay.'

"The ship was given to him with its equipment. We boarded it, we set sail, we arrived at Coptos. It was announced to the priests of Isis of Coptos and the chief priest of Isis. They came down to meet us, hastening to meet Naneferkaptah, and their wives came down to meet me. We went up from the shore and went into the temple of Isis and Harpocrates. Naneferkaptah sent for an ox, a goose, and wine. He made burnt offerings and libations before Isis of Coptos and Harpocrates. We were taken to a very beautiful house filled with all good things.

"Naneferkaptah spent four days making holiday with the priests of Isis of Coptos, and the wives of the priests of Isis made holiday with me. When the morning of our fifth day came, Naneferkaptah had much pure wax brought to him. He made a boat filled with its rowers and sailors. He recited a spell to them, he made them live, he gave them breath, he put them on the water. He filled the ship of Pharaoh with sand, he tied it to the other boat. He went on board, and I sat above the water of Coptos, saying: 'I shall learn what happens to him.'

"He said to the rowers: 'Row me to the place where that book is!' They rowed him all day and all night. In three days he reached it. He cast sand before him, and a gap formed in the river. He found six miles of serpents, scorpions, and all kinds of reptiles around the place where the book was. He found an eternal serpent around this same box. He recited a spell to the six miles of serpents, scorpions, and all kinds of reptiles that were around the box, and did not let them come up. He went to the place where the eternal serpent was. He fought it and killed it. It came to life again and resumed its shape. He fought it again, a second time, and killed it; it came to life again. He fought it again, a third time, cut it in two pieces, and put sand between one piece and the other. It died and no longer resumed its shape.

"Naneferkaptah went to the place where the box was. He found it was a box of iron. He opened it and found a box of copper. He opened it and found a box of juniper wood. He opened it and found a box of ivory and ebony. He opened it and found a box of silver. He opened it and found a box of gold. He opened it and found the book in it. He brought the book up out of the box of gold.

"He recited a spell from it; he charmed the sky, the earth, the netherworld, the mountains, the waters. He discovered what all the birds of the sky and the fish of the deep and the beasts of the desert were saying. He recited another spell; he saw Re appearing in the sky with his Ennead, and the Moon rising, and the stars in their forms. He saw the fish of the deep, though there were twenty-one divine cubits of water over them. He recited a spell to the water; he made it resume its form.

"He went on board, he said to the rowers: 'Row me back to the place I came from.' They rowed him by night as by day. He reached me at the place where I was; he found me sitting above the water of Coptos, not having drunk nor eaten, not having done anything on earth, and looking like a person who has reached the Good House.

"I said to Naneferkaptah: 'Welcome back! Let me see this book for which we have taken these great pains!' He put the book into my hand. I recited one spell from it; I charmed the sky, the earth, the netherworld, the mountains, the waters. I discovered what all the birds of the sky and the fish of the deep and the beasts were saying. I recited another spell; I saw Re appearing in the sky with his Ennead. I saw the Moon rising, and all the stars of the sky in their forms. I saw the fish of the deep, though there were twenty-one divine cubits of water over them.

"As I could not write — I mean, compared with Naneferkaptah, my brother, who was a good scribe and very wise man — he had a sheet of new papyrus brought to him. He wrote on it every word that was in the book before him. He soaked it in beer, he dissolved it in water. When he knew it had dissolved, he drank it and knew what had been in it.

"We returned to Coptos the same day and made holiday before Isis of Coptos and Harpocrates. We went on board, we traveled north, we reached a point six miles north of Coptos.

"Now Thoth had found out everything that had happened to Naneferkaptah regarding the book, and Thoth hastened to report it to Re, saying: 'Learn of my right and my case against Naneferkaptah, the son of King Merneptah! He went to my storehouse; he plundered it; he seized my box with my document. He killed my guardian who was watching over it!

"He was told: 'He is yours together with every person belonging to him.'

"They sent a divine power from heaven, saying: 'Do not allow Naneferkaptah and any person belonging to him to get to Memphis safely!'

"At a certain moment the boy Merib came out from under the awning of the King's ship, fell into the water, and drowned. All the people on board cried out. Naneferkaptah came out from his tent, recited a spell to him, and made him rise up, though there were twenty-one divine cubits of water over him. He recited a spell to him and made him relate to him everything that had happened to him, and the nature of the accusation that Thoth had made before Re.

"We returned to Coptos with him. We had him taken to the Good House. We had him tended, we had him embalmed like a prince and important person. We laid him to rest in his coffin in the desert of Coptos. Naneferkaptah, my brother, said: 'Let us go north, let us not delay, lest the King hear the things that have happened to us and his heart become sad because of them.' We went on board, we went north without delay.

"Six miles north of Coptos, at the place where the boy Merib had fallen into the river, I came out from under the awning of Pharaoh's ship, fell into the river, and drowned. All the people on board cried out and told Naneferkaptah. He came out from the tent of Pharaoh's ship, recited a spell to me, and made me rise up, though there were twenty-one divine cubits of water over me. He had me brought up, recited a spell to me, and made me relate to him everything that had happened to me, and the nature of the accusation that Thoth had made before Re.

"He returned to Coptos with me. He had me taken to the Good House. He had me tended, he had me embalmed in the manner of a prince and a very important person. He laid me to rest in the tomb in which the boy Merib was resting. He went on board, he went north without delay.

"Six miles north of Coptos, at the place where we had fallen into the river, he spoke to his heart saying: 'Could I go to Coptos and dwell there also? If I go to Memphis now and the King asks me about his children, what shall I say to him? Can I say to him, "I took your children to the region of Thebes; I killed them and stayed alive, and I have come to Memphis yet alive?"'

"He sent for a scarf of royal linen belonging to him, and made it into a bandage; he bound the book, placed it on his body, and made it fast. Naneferkaptah came out from under the awning of the King's ship, fell into the water, and drowned. All the people on board cried out, saying: 'Great woe, sad woe! Will he return, the good scribe, the learned man whose like has not been?'

"The King's ship sailed north, no man on earth knowing where Naneferkaptah was. They reached Memphis and sent word to the King. The King came down to meet his ship; he wore mourning dress and all the people of Memphis wore mourning dress, including the priests of Ptah, the chief priest of Ptah, the council, and all the royal household. Then they saw Naneferkaptah holding on to the rudders of Pharaoh's ship through his craft of a good scribe. They brought him up and saw the book on his body.

"The King said: 'Let this book that is on his body be hidden.' Then said the council of Pharaoh and the priests of Ptah and the chief priest of Ptah to the King: 'Our great lord — O may he have the lifetime of Re — Naneferkaptah was a good scribe and a very learned man!' The King had them give him entry into the Good House on the sixteenth day, wrapping on the thirty-fifth, burial on the seventieth day. And they laid him to rest in his coffin in his resting place.

"These are the evil things that befell us on account of this book of which you say, 'Let it be given to me.' You have no claim to it, whereas our lives on earth were taken on account of it!" "So you see," said the boatman. "This is what happens to you when you delve too deeply into knowledge." He tapped a log a few yards away to make sure it was not a crocodile. "Your loved ones get hurt."[1]

"So," I said, "What did Prince Khamwas do?"

"I'll tell you tomorrow," said the boatman. "See, the Sun is setting, and we are far from any big towns. We need to find a place to sleep." He pushed the boat toward the shore, and propelled it onto the sand with his pike. "You are a scribe," he said. "But I trust you do not mind sleeping here, by the River, under the stars?"

---

[1]

"Setna and the Magic Book." *Egypt, Land of Eternity.* https://ib205.tripod.com/book6.html, n.d.

I sat by our fire, watching the waters of the River flow by. The night was blue, the color of Nut in her dreams. The Milky Way of Hathor shone above me. The Heavenly Cow was pacified, she was not in her Lioness form.

The boatman had strummed a few chords on a small-bow harp, and sang some old songs. Then he fell asleep, and was snoring in a pile of tarps he had brought to cover his boat.

I stared out over the water, and my eyes settled on a bobbing light, moving up and down, no bigger than a beetle. It moved this way and that, sometimes against the breeze, until gradually, in an unearthly fashion, it made its way over to me. It grew larger, and settled on the bank in the form of a little boy.

He appeared as Harpocrates, and had a finger to his lips. In reality he was saying, like all children, he wanted to eat. But the Greeks thought that he was keeping a secret, and that he was making an injunction to be silent.

"Hello," I said to the boy. "You look like King Pepi II."

He stuck out a hand to me and beckoned. *Come.*

"Are you Merib? The one who died for the Book of Thoth?"

He nodded. He stamped his foot impatiently.

"Alright," I said. "I'll come with you."

He led me towards the water, to where we had the boat on the bank, moored to a tree.

"What do you want to show me?" I said.

He still had a finger to his lips. He pointed to the water.

"It's Hapi," I said indulgently. "The Great River, and he nourishes us."

He shook his head, and pointed again.

Suddenly the River was lit up with a blue light, which seemed to come from the sky. I could see every fish, every reed and plant — yes, I could see it all down to twenty-one divine cubits of water. And there, at the bottom of the riverbed, I saw the body of a giant serpent, cut in two. "Is that the serpent that your father killed?" I asked Merib.

He nodded. *It is the World Serpent.*

For a moment, I saw the painted sails in the harbor of Alexandria. "The serpent of eternity?"

It is Apep, the one who Ra slays every night.

"My child," I said, "Apep is a being of chaos. Whereas Uraeus-Wadjet protects us, containing all."

Apep and Uraeus-Wadjet are one. This is the nature

of the difference between inside, and outside.

"So you are saying…"

Look to eternity. There are two forms of time.

"The soul both transmigrates, and it abides."

Yes, the child nodded, finger still upon his lips. Then he beckoned me to bend down and he whispered something in my ear.

This is the Word, he said.

I forgot about this encounter until the next day, when I was sitting in the barge. Then suddenly, as on a wind, I heard this Word come back to me, settling upon my tongue. The boatman and I had not said much to each other. We had passed some friends of his earlier that day, reed-makers, and had chatted with them for a while before continuing on. Now we sat in silence, passing farms and villages on either side of the river.

The Word was on my tongue. I felt it there, tasted it, enjoyed its presence all the more knowing that I was about to use it. Then, I stood up inside my body, looked through Time, and said it.

I saw Re appearing in the sky with his Ennead. I saw the Moon rising, and all the stars of the sky in their forms. I saw the fish of the deep, though there were twenty-one divine cubits of water over them. I was above my body, high on a road in the sky. There was the Ennead, and they were written upon the World Serpent. I looked up, and I could see the celestial spheres rising above me, each one a snake devouring its own tail. Then I saw in the center all of it, even the Sun, orbited an Eternal Fire, a Flame Imperishable that seemed unmoving. There was the Serpent that encircled all, that contained within itself its own beginning and ending.

This was time, the boy had said. But what was the other form of time, if there are two of them? The soul transmigrates; certainly, it revolves endlessly around its circle, taking form after form. But where does it *abide?* Suddenly, I wanted to know. The taste of the forbidden was on my tongue. I made my thought into an arrow, I made it cutting like a dagger. I looked upon the boundaries of eternity, I looked at the very World Serpent itself.

If this is Inside...what is Outside? And I cut through the World Serpent with my Mind, trying to see what could be on the other side, in the impossible.

Blackness. Pain, stabbing, between my eyes and in my ears. Blackness blacker than the ink that I wrote in demotic. As though there were things, *entities*, in the Outside, that wanted to consume, which hungered. Wriggling like the tails of a thousand scorpions.

Suddenly I felt a sense of alarm. I pulled my eye away from what I was looking at and looked down. Far, far below me, under a sea of stars, I saw the Earth, and the river Hapi. Very small like an ant upon it was our boat, and I saw that the boatman had fallen off his perch and into the water. I sped back towards my body as quickly as possible, passing back down through the Ennead into the sky and the eaves of Egypt, racing along with the wind.

I crashed back into my body, almost falling into the river myself. Our boat had started to flow downstream. I grabbed the pike and stuck it in the mud, anchoring it to the ground. Then I dove in the water, searching for the plume of the boatman's robes. I could see nothing in the water. Everything was murk. What could I...the Word came back to me again. I spoke it, and it bubbled out of my mouth to the surface of the water.

I charmed the sky, the earth, the netherworld, the mountains, the waters. I discovered what all the birds of the sky and the fish of the deep and the beasts were saying. I saw through the murk in the water, and I grabbed his hand. I grabbed him from underneath twenty-one divine cubits of water, and I pulled him up.

I pulled him up and threw him out on the bank. He spluttered and coughed and shook out his hair.

"You idiot scholar," he gasped to me. "I told you the story to warn you *not* to do the spell!"

We did not sail any more that day. I swam back out to the boat and rowed it to shore, and we moored it to the husk of a palm.

The boatman was wheezing from his ordeal so I built him a fire. It was one of those mercurial days where even in the hot it is still possible to catch cold. While I built the fire he lectured me.

"You are the kind of person," he said, "who sees a burning building, and then next to it there is a robber who says to him 'Come inside' and you trust the robber and ignore the building!"

I was silent, and piled a few more pieces of bark in the dust.

"What did you think you were trying to accomplish? I felt the Gods come down upon us."

I blew on some coals. "So," I said at last. "The Book of Thoth is not, actually, a book."

He gaped at me. "Yes! Obviously! That is the whole point. But did you really have to cut through the whole of reality before you figured that out?"

"It's out here," I said, gesturing.

"It is in the silence of the Ibis, the nourishment of the Crocodile, the ardor of the Jackal, and the rampage of the Hippopotamus. It is in the very waters of the River itself!"

"Beneath the River," I said, finally getting it to light.

"In the whole of Creation," said the boatman. "The Book of Thoth is not any one piece of knowledge. It is a way of *seeing*."

"Explain," I said.

"Haha," he said. "He almost drowns me and then he says 'Explain.' Listen to the messages that Nature has for you. Everything is a message, everything can be interpreted. Ta-tanen is always trying to disclose something to us."

"So it's a way of interpretation?" I said.

"No, because the universe is not just a book! I will tell you the end of the story, maybe then you will understand."

Setne said to Ahwere: "Let me have this book that I see between you and Naneferkaptah, or else I will take it by force!"

Naneferkaptah rose from the bier and said: "Are you Setne, to whom this woman has told these dire things and you have not accepted them? The said book, will you be able to seize it through the power of a good scribe, or through skill in playing draughts with me? Let the two of us play draughts for it!"

Said Setne, "I am ready."

They put before them the game board with its pieces, and they both played. Naneferkaptah won one game from Setne. He recited a spell to him, struck his head with the game-box that was before him, and made him sink into the ground as far as his legs.

He did the same with the second game. He won it from Setne, and made him sink into the ground as far as his phallus. He did the same with the third game, and made him sink into the ground as far as his ears. After this Setne was in great straits at the hands of Naneferkaptah.

Setne called to his foster-brother Inaros, saying: "Hasten up to the earth and tell Pharaoh everything that has happened to me; and bring the amulets of my father Ptah and my books of sorcery."

He hastened up to the earth and told Pharaoh everything that had happened to Setne.

Pharaoh said: "Take him the amulets of his father Ptah and his books of sorcery."

Inaros hastened down into the tomb. He put the amulets on the body of Setne, and he jumped up in that very moment. Setne stretched out his hand for the book and seized it.

Then, as Setne came up from the tomb, light went before him, darkness went behind him, and Ahwere wept after him, saying: "Hail, O darkness! Farewell, O light! Everything that was in the tomb has departed!"

Naneferkaptah said to Ahwere: "Let your heart not grieve. I will make him bring this book back here, with a forked stick in his hand and a lighted brazier on his head!"

Setne came up from the tomb and made it fast behind him, as it had been. Setne went before Pharaoh and related to him the things that had happened to him on account of the book.

The King said to Setne: "Take this book back to the

tomb of Naneferkaptah like a wise man, or else he will make you take it back with a forked stick in your hand and a lighted brazier on your head."

Setne did not listen to him. Then Setne had no occupation on earth but to unroll the book and read from it to everyone.

After this it happened one day that Setne was strolling in the forecourt of the temple of Ptah. Then he saw a woman who was very beautiful, there being no other woman like her in appearance. She was beautiful and wore many golden jewels, and maid servants walked behind her as well as two men servants belonging to her household.

The moment Setne saw her, he did not know where on earth he was.

He called his man servant, saying: "Hasten to the place where this woman is, and find out what her position is." The man servant hastened to the place where the woman was.

He called to the maid servant who was following her and asked her, saying, "What woman is this?"

She told him: "It is Tabubu, the daughter of the prophet of Bastet, mistress of Ankhtawi. She has come here to worship Ptah, the great god."

The servant returned to Setne and related to him every word she had said to him.

Setne said to the servant: "Go, say to the maid, 'It is Setne Khamwas, the son of King Usermare, who has sent me to say, "I will give you ten pieces of gold-spend an hour with me. Or do you have a complaint of wrongdoing? I will have it settled for you. I will have you taken to a hidden place where no one on earth shall find you." ' "

The servant returned to the place where Tabubu was. He called her maid and told her.

She cried out as if what he said was an insult. Tabubu said to the servant: "Stop talking to this foolish maid; come and speak with me."

The servant hastened to where Tabubu was and said to her: "I will give you ten pieces of gold; spend an hour with Setne Khamwas, the son of King Usermare. If you have a complaint of wrongdoing, he will have it settled for you. He will take you to a hidden place where no one on earth shall find you."

Tabubu said: "Go, tell Setne, 'I am of priestly rank, I am not a low person. If you desire to do what you wish with me, you must come to Bubastis, to my house. It is furnished with everything, and you shall do what you wish with me, without anyone on earth finding me and without my acting like a low woman of the street.' "

The servant returned to Setne and told him everything she had said to him. He said, "That suits me!" Everyone around Setne was indignant.

Setne had a boat brought to him. He went on board and hastened to Bubastis. When he came to the west of the suburb he found a very lofty house that had a wall around it, a garden on its north, and a seat at its door.

Setne asked, "Whose house is this?"

They told him, "It is the house of Tabubu."

Setne went inside the wall. While he turned his face to the storehouse in the garden they announced him to Tabubu. She came down, took Setne's hand, and said to him: "By the welfare of the house of the prophet of Bastet, mistress of Ankhtawi, which you have reached, it will please me greatly if you will take the trouble to come up with me."

Setne walked up the stairs of the house with Tabubu. He found the upper story of the house swept and adorned, its floor adorned with real lapis-lazuli and real turquoise. Many couches were in it, spread with royal linen, and many golden cups were on the table. A golden cup was filled with wine and put into Setne's hand.

She said to him, "May it please you to eat something."

He said to her, "I could not do that."

Incense was put on the brazier; ointment was brought to him of the kind provided for Pharaoh. Setne made holiday with Tabubu, never having seen anyone like her.

Setne said to Tabubu: "Let us accomplish what we have come here for."

She said to him: "You will return to your house in which you live. I am of priestly rank; I am not a low person. If you desire to do what you wish with me you must make for me a deed of maintenance and of compensation in money for everything, all goods belonging to you."

He said to her: "Send for the school teacher."

He was brought at once. He made for her a deed of maintenance and of compensation in money for everything, all goods belonging to him.

At this moment one came to announce to Setne, "Your children are below."

He said, "Let them be brought up." Tabubu rose and put on a garment of royal linen. Setna saw all her limbs through it, and his desire became even greater than it had been before.

Setne said: "Tabubu, let me accomplish what I have come here for!"

She said to him: "You will return to your house in which you live. I am of priestly rank; I am not a low person. If you desire to do what you wish with me, you must make your children subscribe to my deed. Do not leave them to contend with my children over your property."

He had his children brought and made them subscribe to the deed.

Setne said to Tabubu: "Let me accomplish what I have come for!"

She said to him: "You will return to your house in which you live. I am of priestly rank; I am not a low person. If you desire to do what you wish with me, you must have your children killed. Do not leave them to contend with my children over your property."

Setne said: "Let the abomination that came into your head be done to them."

She had his children killed before him. She had them thrown down from the window to the dogs and cats. They ate their flesh, and he heard them as he drank with Tabubu.

Setne said to Tabubu: "Let us accomplish what we have come here for! All the things that you have said, I have done them all for you."

She said to him: "Come now to this storehouse."

Setne went to the storehouse. He lay down on a couch of ivory and ebony, his wish about to be fulfilled. Tabubu lay down beside Setne. He stretched out his hand to touch her, and she opened her mouth wide in a loud cry. Setne awoke in a state of great heat, his phallus ragingly erect, and there were no clothes on him at all.

At this moment Setne saw a noble person born in a litter, with many men running beside him, and he had the likeness of Pharaoh. Setne was about to rise but could not rise for shame because he had no clothes on.

Pharaoh said: "Setne, what is this state that you are in?"

He said: "It is Naneferkaptah who has done it all to me!" Pharaoh said: "Go to Memphis; your children want you; they stand in their rank before Pharaoh."

Setne said to Pharaoh: "My great lord - O may he have the lifetime of Re."

Pharaoh called to a servant who was standing by and

made him give clothes to Setne. Pharaoh said: "Setne, go to Memphis; your children are alive; they stand in their rank before Pharaoh."

When Setne came to Memphis he embraced his children, for he found them alive.

The King said to Setne: "Was it a state of drunkenness you were in before?"

Setne related everything that had happened with Tabubu and Naneferkaptah.

The King said: "Setne, I did what I could with you before, saying, 'They will kill you if you do not take this book back to the place you took it from.' You have not listened to me until now. Take this book back to Naneferkaptah, with a forked stick in your hand and a lighted brazier on your head."

When Setne came out from before the King, there was a forked stick in his hand and a lighted brazier on his head. He went down into the tomb in which Naneferkaptah was.

Ahwere said to him: "Setne, it is the great god Ptah who has brought you back safely."

Naneferkaptah laughed, saying, "It is what I told you before."

Setne greeted Naneferkaptah, and he found one could say that Pre was in the whole tomb. Ahwere and Naneferkaptah greeted Setne warmly.

Setne said: "Naneferkaptah, is there any matter

which is shameful?"

Naneferkaptah said: "Setne, you know that Ahwere and her son Merib are in Coptos; here in this tomb they are through the craft of a good scribe. Let it be asked of you to undertake the task of going to Coptos and bringing them here."

When Setne had come up from the tomb, he went before Pharaoh and related to Pharaoh everything that Naneferkaptah had said to him.

Pharaoh said: "Setne, go to Coptos, bring Ahwere and her son Merib."

He said to Pharaoh: "Let the ship of Pharaoh and its equipment be given to me."

The ship of Pharaoh and its equipment were given to him. He went on board, he set sail, he reached Coptos without delay. It was announced to the priests of Isis of Coptos, and the chief priest of Isis. They came down to meet him, they conducted him to the shore.

He went up from it, he went into the temple of Isis of Coptos and Harpocrates. He sent for an ox, a goose, and wine, and made burnt offerings and libation before Isis of Coptos and Harpocrates. He went to the desert of Coptos with the priests of Isis and the chief priest of Isis. They spent three days and three nights searching in all the tombs on the desert of Coptos, turning over the stelae of the scribes of the House of Life, and reading the inscriptions on them. They did not find the resting place in which Ahwere and her son were.

When Naneferkaptah found that they did not find the resting place of Ahwere and her son Merib, he rose up as an old man, a very aged priest, and came to meet Setne. When Setne saw him he said to the old man: "You have the appearance of a man of great age. Do you know the resting place in which Ahwere and her son Merib are?"

The old man said to Setne: "My great-grandfather said to my grandfather, 'The resting place of Ahwere and her son Merib is at the south corner of the house of the chief of police.' "

Setne said to the old man: "Perhaps there is some wrong that the chief of police did to you, on account of which you are trying to have his house torn down?"

The old man said to Setne: "Have a watch set over me, and let the house of the chief of police be demolished. If they do not find Ahwere and her son Merib under the south corner of his house, let punishment be done to me."

They set a watch over the old man, and they found the resting place of Ahwere and her son Merib under the south corner of the house of the chief of police.

Setne let the two noble persons enter into Pharaoh's ship. He had the house of the chief of police built as it had been before.

Naneferkaptah let Setne learn the fact that it was he who had come to Coptos, to let them find the resting place in which Ahwere and her son Merib were.

Setne went on board Pharaoh's ship. He went north and without delay he reached Memphis with all the people who were with him. When it was announced before Pharaoh, he came down to meet the ship of Pharaoh. He let the noble persons enter into the tomb in which Naneferkaptah was. He had it closed over them all together.It was night. The boatman had stopped speaking, and was lying next to the fire. "And that, scribe, is why one should not be too greedy for knowledge. Do you understand?"

"It was a good story," I said.

"Knowledge..." said the boatman, yawning, "knowledge is like a beautiful woman..." and then he fell asleep.

The next day we came to the outskirts of a large city.

"Where is this?" I asked him.

"Khemenu," he said. "City of the 8. I go no further from here."

"Why not?" I said, wishing to put as much distance between me and Alexandria as possible.

"Because it is on the border between Lower and Upper Egypt," he said. "And I do not go to Upper Egypt. I told you."

"You said you did not go South, but you did not tell me why."

"I do not like Thebes," said the boatman. "Or Thebans. I agree with Ahwere on that count. Thebes is a place of misery for me."

"Well then what am I to do?" I said.

"You are a scribe," said the boatman. "I would suggest you seek employment at the local temple. You can write in hieroglyphs, not just the Greek language, right?"

"Some..." I said.

"You know why this city is called Khemenu?"

Come on. "Yes elder," I said. "Because of the Ogdo-ad. 'The City of the 8.' I am not a child."

"You are not a child but you have gone Greek. Do you remember the names of the 8 Gods and Goddesses of Infinity?"

"Why are you quizzing me?" I said. "Nu and Naunet, the abysmal, Hehu and Hehut, the uncountable, Kekui and Kekuit, darkness, Qerh and Qerhet, the inherent. What kind of boatman are you, that you quiz your passengers about theology, and lecture them about the dangers of magic?"

"Do you remember," he said, "when Isis tricked Re into giving her his secret name?"

"Yes," I said, "she made an adder out of spit and it poisoned him in the sky. She made a serpent of chaos which split the World Serpent. Or they are one and the same. Then she tricked him."

"Then watch out," he said laughing, "or this simple, uneducated boatman will get ahold of your secret name! Luckily for you, you've had the sense to not even tell me your name. Tell me my friend, are you a fugitive?"

"No," I said. "I'm visiting family."

"All Egyptians are family," said the boatman.

"That's right," I said.

We came around a bend in the river, and I saw in the

distance a large fortress with white spires, rising from a promontory of red rock. "What is that?" I said.

"That is the castle of Hermopolis Magna," said the boatman. "And, incidentally, the place where the Thebans take their tolls. Even under the Greeks, this city is still truly theirs. We are not stopping there. We are stopping at the docks in the center of the city."

"Do you have something against the god Ammon?" I joked. This was the God of Thebes, and the one who leant the Thebans their power.

The boatman did not say anything, but kept guiding the small barge upriver. I thought of Naneferekapah's wife and son, drowned in the River at Coptos.

"Do you have any family?" I asked.

"Not now," he said. "Not when you almost drowned me."

Khemenu, which the Greeks call Hermopolis, was taller than either Memphis or Alexandria. Most of the buildings rose more than five stories, and were an amalgam of hodge-podge mudbrick construction. By some consensus of the inhabitants the houses were painted either blue, yellow, or white, and it gave the impression of entering a giant stone forest made of lazuli and gold.

"Over there," said the boatman, pointing. "That is the Gate of the Moon, the largest thoroughfare into or out of the city, excepting the River of course."

"The Gate of the Moon," I said. "You have brought me to the city of the god Thoth."

"Of course," said the boatman. "That is what you were looking for."

"After your stories I'm not sure I want to look any longer."

"You will," he said. "It's in your nature." We entered

a sea of boats and activity as we came towards the docks. "It may be a while before we get a berth," he said.

"How much do I owe you?" I said.

"What?" he said. "Don't be ridiculous, I was going this way anyways."

"All the same," I said. "I would like to give you something for your trouble."

"If you must," he said. "But I am delivering letters and selling goods here, so I'll be fine."

"No," I said, "for the lesson." I held out the ostracon with the prayers to Osiris written on it.

"Why are you giving me this?" he said.

"My father gave it to me," I said. "When he came back from his pilgrimage to Abydos."

"This is a very important thing you are giving a boatman."

"This is the only pilgrimage I will ever take."

He stared me dead in the eye. "That, I think is unlikely."

"All the same, thank you."

"I accept," he said, taking the ostracon. "And I was wrong about you. You are made of sterner stuff than you appear."

We moored, and then parted, leaving me alone in Khemenu: city of the 8 Infinities. The last thing the boatman said was to again recommend I take my service to the temple; but I still wanted to try my hand at being an independent scribe.

I went to a tavern by the side of the river, and ordered some beer. When it came it was Egyptian country-beer, of the kind I had not had since my childhood - more bread than water, ideal for long days working under the Sun. I sat there, taking in the scene, trying to get a feel for the city that I had found myself in, and where it would be best for me to sell my services. Most of the people in here were old men, the kind who would not be working in the middle of the day during the Emergence Season. It was the ideal time to be sowing.

And at that moment, my career as an independent scribe ended.

I overheard one of the patrons, speaking into his beer: "So the runner said that this fugitive, who poisoned half of the cows in the Greek city, has come down here?"

"Yes, we are to watch the river for one with Greek mannerisms and an educated bearing. He will come as a scribe, and have a Saiite name," said another.

"Does it really matter," said an attendant, setting down a plate of barley for a patron and joining the conversation briefly, "what happens in the Greek City? All it means is that, for want of food and milk, from us they will take more grain."

"It matters to the Castle Guard down south," said one of the men, old with a wispy beard. "They are offering a hefty reward for the capture of this person. Apparently he defied the King and broke out of jail."

"Defiance," said the attendant. "The worst of sins."

"I don't know," said the other patron, "they say the heart has its own demands — from what I've heard he said, I don't know if I could have spoken otherwise." The other two stared at him.

"Well," said the attendant. "You said there is a reward? We're close to the river. I'll keep watch."

I left some coins on the table — too much for the beer — and left the harbor district.

The Temple was huge, one of the largest I had ever seen. Even the massive monuments of Ramses Usermaare in Memphis barely compared to this. And to think this was built by the Greek Kings. The columns of its forecourt were painted in bright bands of red, yellow, and blue. Surrounding the precincts was a retaining wall, rising but not entirely obscuring the jumble of white and yellow buildings surrounding it. I could see why they kept the world out: inside the temple grounds was one of the most beautiful and peaceful gardens I had ever seen.

There was a guard out front. "Who are you?" he said. "And are you coming to make an offering?"

"My name is Kaires," I said. "And I am a scribe, coming to offer myself to this temple."

"Kaires," said the guard. "You are named after the Sage Kaires? That is a bold name for a scribe."

"My father was a proud man," I said. What had

Kaires written again? I had spent so long trying to be Greek, it was true, I was close to forgetting my own literature.

"From your speech," said the guard, "it sounds like you come from the Delta. What are you doing this far South?"

"I am a wandering scholar," I said. "Can I speak to the high priest of this temple, or, is there anyone in charge?"

"He is so busy," said the guard. "And I'm sorry, I can see that you're educated, but I can't let just anyone in."

"Couldn't you take a message?"

"I suppose," said the guard. "But you know we have a lot of people who can write here, so you would really have to have some other purpose. We're not hiring right now."

I stood there, feeling the urgency of my own situation, trying to find some way to ask for asylum without asking for asylum. I could go back to the harbor and charter another boat South, but there was a problem — that Castle, from which my friend said the Thebans took a toll. And the men in the tavern had been talking about a reward the Castle Guard were offering. Going back North was suicide, so it seemed I was stuck on the border between Lower Egypt and Upper Egypt, unable to go either way. Unless I pulled a Sinuhe and went out to the desert to join the Sand-farers, but that seemed unlikely.

The guard seemed to pick up on something. "Let's see," he said. "I can see you are a good man. Bentreshyt!" he called.

There was a rustling in the garden, and then a woman emerged from between the geraniums, lilies, lotuses and papyrus bushes. She was the most beautiful woman I had ever seen.

I cannot describe her to you. It is not just that her appearance was beautiful, that her limbs and body were perfect, that she moved with a natural grace, elegance and self-possession I had never seen before. No, it was not just that. It was that she had all these things, and that inside, her spirit, was beautiful too. The instant I looked at her I was enchanted. I knew she was casting a spell, and I did not care.

"Hello," she said. "Who is this?"

"Kaires," said the guard. "The sage-scribe."

"Oh my," she said, laughing. "Well that's a good name."

"I have come to offer my services to the temple."

"Ah," she said. "What do you write? Demotic, hieratic, or hieroglyphs?"

"Well, demotic mostly," I admitted. "But I do have some hieroglyphs. Not much though."

"Hmm," she said. "We already have plenty of people who write demotic. Too many, in fact. Have you tried the Castle? They always need people to write their registry." She turned as if she was about to go.

"Not the Castle," I said. "I mean, I don't want to work in a secular capacity. I want to pledge myself to a God." She turned back to me, interested. "And I know my education is a bit abnormal, but I can also write in Greek."

"You write Greek?" she said. "That is interesting. We do not have anyone here writing in Greek. I do not know what we would use it for."

"There is an opportunity," I said, "to make our religion comprehensible to the foreigners. At least, this is what I have devoted my life to. It may seem strange, but I have spent my whole life trying to translate a book about Imhotep commissioned by King Nectanebo II himself."

"Imhotep!" she said. "That is interesting. Very, very interesting, the work you are doing. Let me go speak to Ammonius," she said, "our High Priest. Can you wait in the Hypostyle Hall? I'll get you an audience. Thank you Idem," she said to the guard.

She turned to go and then turned back. "Do you have a copy of this book of King Nectanebo of Sais with you?"

"Well, no," I said. "I lost it years ago."

"Then," she said, "how do you propose to make a translation?"

"I have written the beginning of my account, at the behest of the God. But I was prevented from completing it by misfortune."

"That is...strange," she said. "All the same we are devoted to the God here. Imhotep. If he favors you, then I will speak to our High Priest." She left and walked up the steps, and entered the temple.

199

The guard gestured to me. "Just go stand there in the forecourt and wait for them to come out."

"Thank you," I said. I walked up the steps, passing through the dual gate, and went into the Hypostyle Hall. The colors here were also red, yellow and blue, but overlaid on the massive columns — each one easily twenty times my size — were a series of hieroglyphs. The sedge and the bee. Djed, was and ankh. There was someone's nebty name, who was it? Could I still read? P-t-l-m, S-t-r... Ptolemy Soter. The savior. The first Greek King. It was him, then, who commissioned this temple.

Then I saw a very old man with a long white beard coming through the far court, walking very quickly. Bentreshyt was not far behind, trying to keep up. He was pointing at me, and hauling up his robes as he walked.

"You, boy!" he said. "Are you an icthyophagoi?"

What the? "Am I a fish-eater?" I said. Oh. He was trying to ask me if I was ritually pure, not whether I was an inhabitant of the Far Hijaz. "No, Father," I said. "No, I do not eat fish."

"Good," he said. "My name is Ammonius. Welcome to our temple."

"There are fewer and fewer left," said the High Priest. "We used to have much greater wisdom than we have now. But you have a good name. Bentreshyt tells me you carry the name Kaires."

I fingered my cup of wine uncomfortably, trying not to let on that I had forgotten what it was that prophet had written. We were sitting in a small room off the temple precinct with some tables, where it seemed the temple attendants ate.

"I used to read the *Instruction of Kagemni* every day. It brought me guidance in dark times."

"Kagemni..." I said, "was Kaires' son?"

"Yes my child," said Ammonius. "And he lived during the reign of King Teti, long ago in the time of the pyramids."

"I have a question for you, Father," I said. "On my way here, I heard a story about Setne Khamwas, whom we call Khaemwaset, who discovered a Book of Thoth in a tomb outside Memphis. Is there any truth to this story?"

"I think I know the story you are talking about," he said. "It is very popular. The story of Naneferkaptah?"

"Yes, that's the one."

"Well," he said. "You mean if there actually was a 'Book of Thoth' buried outside Memphis, and the Prince dug it up? Khaemwaset was famous for such things. We have much to thank him for. I think that the restoration of many temples and monuments in his Father's reign - a thousand years ago, now - was due in part to his passion for digging up old tombs and monuments, and exploring the past for secret knowledge. Sometimes to the chagrin of his contemporaries."

"But Merneptah was his brother, right?"

"Very good, you know the King Lists," said Ammonius. "Yes, Merneptah was his brother."

"So then," I said, "what is the Book of Thoth?"

He was silent for a while. "You are talking to a priest of Thoth, but in this temple, we also honor Ammon. From this comes my name: I have pledged my life to this God. But you know, there are older Gods. Gods from long before the time of Khaemwaset. In this city we are devoted to some of the oldest Gods in existence: the Ogdoad."

"I have been driven a very long way," I said. "Pursued by the spirit of Imhotep."

"It makes sense," said Ammonius, "that one such as you, bearing the name Kaires, should be pursued by Imhotep."

"It does?" I said.

"Yes. Because Imhotep was the first philosopher, and he wrote the first sebayt. *The Instruction of Imhotep.*"

"I did not know," I said, "that Imhotep wrote a sebayt."

"Clearly, in the North you have forgotten. But Lower Egypt has always been decadent, since the beginning of time, and you have always needed Upper Egypt to come rescue you."

"Can I read this book?" I said.

"We have a copy of it in the Temple library," said Ammonius. "I cannot believe that you have come all this way to translate a book about the Prophet written for one of your Saiite Kings, and yet you have not even bothered to do the first thing and read what Imhotep actually wrote. It is shameful!"

"Well," I said truthfully. "Call it a lapse in my education, but I had not heard of it before."

"Where would you Northerners be?" he asked, staring at me, "If King Menes had not rescued you from yourselves? You would be carousing like a bunch of Asiatics!"

"Father," I said, "with respect, we are not truly in Upper Egypt, no? Hermopolis - Khemenu - is on the border."

He pounded the table, shaking the cups and bowls, and nearly shaking me. "This has always been Ammon's country!" he said. "You do not understand, man from Sais, with a name that is too good for you, what it is we have had to do."

"And that is?" I said.

"We keep the faith alive," he said. "Now listen. I want to see how your hieroglyphs are, because if you can only read small sentences we may not be able to keep you here. You are welcome to consult the library — in fact I *encourage* you to, because we do not need anyone making a false translation — but I do not know how long we can retain your services, Kaires."

My heart sank. If I could not stay here, I was in great danger. "My hieroglyphs are not so bad, sir."

"Good," said Ammonius. "I will give you a book in demotic and ask you to transcribe it in Hieroglyphics and Hieratic. The training book. The book of 'The House of Life.'"

I was in the Temple Scriptorium, staring at a copy of *The Chamber of Darkness.* It was in demotic, and I had seen it before. When they had sent me to the temple of Neith as a child, this was the book I had used to learn how to write. It was the book every young scribe used. It consisted of a conversation between a master, "The One of Hereset", or Thoth - I realized now that Hereset was here, the necropolis of Thoth in Khemenu, a detail which as a child I had always passed over - and "The One Who Loves Knowledge", the initiate, the student who is trying to learn.

The One Who Loves Knowledge says:
Behold, Hu, Divine Utterance
Behold, Sia, Divine Insight
Seeing and hearing:
The Butler of the Sacred Books, of the Ba-souls.

It was with Hu that I had conquered the Ennead, and cut through the World Serpent. And it was Sia that had allowed me to come back to Earth, and rescue the boatman in time. How did you write Sia again? Well, you could use different letters, but you always wrote it with the symbol of a man pointing his thumb towards his mouth. The symbol a child uses to say it wanted to eat, and a grown man uses to indicate he has something to say. The Word. I wrote the symbol for 's'.

Bentreshyt came into the room, glancing over my shoulder.

"Oh!" she cried. "So you *can* write hieroglyphs!"

"Not that well," I said. "This is just scratches."

"Well it seems very good to me," she said. She sat down across from me at the table. "So tell me," she said. "What brings a pilgrim of Imhotep all the way here from the North?"

"I'm looking for the Holy Knowledge," I said. 'The Book of Thoth."

"But you have it right in front of you," she said.

"What? *The Chamber of Darkness?*"

"No, silly. Sia. The Word in your heart."

I was a bit frustrated with her, that she would outsmart me so quickly. "Which God are you pledged to then?" I said to her, perhaps too sharply.

She shook her head. "I am not pledged to a God. I am pledged to Seshat, the Goddess of Writing." She picked up my transliteration. "And I believe Seshat thinks you have done a good job."

"Who is this Seshat?" I asked.

"She is the wife of Thoth."

"I thought Thoth was married to Ma'at. I mean, I thought Truth was married to Justice."

"It depends," said Bentreshyt. "On your interpretation of the divine hall of records. Some say Thoth is married to Ma'at. But in the old days, in the time before time, everyone knew that Thoth was married to Seshat. He was the one who loved knowledge, the reed pen. She was the glyph he wrote, the form that contained him."

I stared at her. I put my pen down.

"Did you know," she said. "That Imhotep had two daughters?"

She led me to a side-chapel beside the Hypostyle Hall. It was surrounded by a small canal of still-water, within which lotuses flourished. She had with her a broom made of rushes, and she was bent over, sweeping the ground as she walked.

"This is the chapel of Imhotep and his family," she said. She swept some sycamore leaves from the threshold of the door. "Please," she said. "If it pleases the Gods, enter." I stepped through the door, and entered a small white room covered in hieroglyphs. I could see the names of King Zoser, and the ancestors from the time of the pyramids, written in a list down one wall. Bentreshyt stepped in after me, and led me to a statue on the front wall of the chapel.

There was the Prophet Imhotep, flanked on either side by two women: one older, the other younger, and slim. Between the legs of the three adults stood two small girls.

"This," said Bentreshyt, gesturing to the woman on

the left of Imhotep, "is the mother of Imhotep. Her name was Khereduankh, and we worship her now as the Mother of God." She gestured to the smaller, slimmer woman on the right. "This is Renpetneferet. His mystic sister. His wife. In Greek she is called Hygieia."

"Were they actually brother and sister?" I asked.

"Well," said Bentreshyt. "That also depends on your opinion." She was smiling. "Renpetneferet is sacred to Seshat."

"Did she know how to write?" I asked.

"You will have to ask her," said Bentreshyt. She touched her left breast. The gesture a woman uses when a child wants to nurse, or when she is trying hard to keep her speech holy.

"How?" I asked. "Is there an Oracle?"

"The cult of the family is alive," she said. "They still make offerings to them at the City of the Dead. But I had promised to show you the beautiful ones. These are Imhotep's two daughters."

"Who was Imhotep's Father?" I asked.

"Kanofer," she said. "An architect. But you will have to ask Ammonius about that. He knows more than me. And about his brother, Amenhotep son of Hapu."

"Imhotep had a brother?"

"Spiritual brothers," said Bentreshyt. "Amenhotep son of Hapu lived more than a thousand years after Imhotep, and that was more than a thousand years ago. He was alive in the reign of the king Amenhotep III"

"Amenophis," I breathed.

"Sorry?" she said.

"Just the name a teacher of mine, a priest named Manetho, uses."

"I imagine you pronounce things differently in the Delta."

"Yes..." I got lost in the carvings, looking at the story of the little family, rising from the place of commoners, to being deified as Gods.

She was looking at me.

"You know," she said. "Imhotep was originally a priest of Ptah, but he has become one with Thoth in divinity. Renpetneferet was a priestess of Bast, but she has become one with Seshat."

"What do you mean?"

"I mean..." she started twirling her broom. "I mean that the path to divinity is not always straightforward. It does not always lead where you expect." She looked sad.

"Why did you say you could not write Hieroglyphs?" said Ammonius. "This is better than half of the scribes I hire from around the city, and this is the city of Thoth, for crying out loud."

"Where I come from, in Sais," I said, "this is not considered very good."

"No?" said Ammonius.

"No, especially not compared to the wonder that came before us. And I have not practiced hieroglyphs for a long time."

"Well, it is certainly enough for me to justify employing you to the tax office. You have an interesting style too."

"Perhaps it is because" I said, barely suppressing a smile, "We Northerners will always outshine you Southerners, in our grace and sophistication."

"Whereas to you," said Ammonius, "I probably look like a country bumpkin. Well, isn't it so. One can never look through the eyes of a God."

"Father," I said. "I wanted to ask you something about that, actually. This Amenhotep son of Hapu."

"Yes?" he said.

"What was his history? I have heard that he it was who helped King Amenhotep III throw out Moses, the King of the Lepers."

"Ah," said Ammonius. "The Heretic. We do not say his name."

"Moses?" I said.

"That will do," said Ammonius. "Because that is not his actual name."

"Only I had heard," I said. "That Amenhotep, son of Hapu, is the spiritual brother to Imhotep."

"That is true," said Ammonius. "On several counts: they were both architects, they were both commoners, they were both scribes, and in much the same way, they ascended to Godhood within their own lifetime. In that sense they are the ideal of what an Egyptian sage should be."

"But what is the history of this Amenhotep son of Hapu? And who is this Heretic which he opposed?"

"For that," said Ammonius, "You must understand the history of Thebes, and the history of my God Ammon. But it is a history of terrible things. My son, what do you know of Hyksos?"

"I have learned much of them from my teacher Manetho," I said. "They came from Canaan, from the land of the Jews. They invaded and held all of Egypt hostage. They pillaged the temples. They destroyed the entire country. Egypt was never the same again."

"Yes," said Ammonius. "But who drove them out?"

I had never thought of this. "I don't know."

"Another question," said Ammonius. "From which city did King Amenhotep III, whom you asked about, rule?"

"Well, Thebes, I guess," I said. "He ruled from Upper Egypt."

"And what is the God of Thebes?"

"The God of Thebes is Ammon."

"Correct," said Ammonius. "The force which drove the Hyksos out of the country was the Priesthood of the God Ammon, a Sacred Order."

"I do not understand what this has to do with Amenhotep son of Hapu, or with the Heretic King."

"You see, it has everything to do with this King. The Jews claim that this King was their prophet, Moses. They say that the heresy that he established was like the worship of their God, in their religion. But they do not understand this. The truth of the matter is, there was a power struggle between the Kings and the Priests of my Order, after we expelled the Hyksos. The Kings lost."

"What do you mean?" I said. "I thought that all priests supported the Divine Kingship?"

"Come now, Kaires, you are from Sais. You have seen all of the corruptions of power that are gotten up to there.

Let me tell you what actually happened.

"We saved Egypt, when we drove the Hyksos out, but at a cost. If you want to understand it roughly, there were two factions. One was the faction which wanted to build an Empire. We thought that the best way to protect Egypt was for it to conquer land in Asia, and become like the Asiatics, so that we would prevent another Hyksos invasion to occur. This was especially popular in the army, where the worship of Set became commonplace. It was thought that our country would have to turn to that black power now for its own self defense. This is the side that my Order, the Priesthood of Ammon, took."

"But this is not a good thing," I said. "It is falling into the worship of Chaos."

"Yes," said Ammonius, "and that is what the other side said. They were less organized than we were, but they were chiefly those of the Royalty. See, there were three parts of our government in the old time: the Priesthood, the Army, and the Kings. In this case, the Priesthood and the Army allied against the Kings, who wanted to keep to the old ways. This started a struggle which happened long before the King the Jews called Moses."

"So your Order," I said, "the Theban Priests of Amun, conspired to overthrow the throne."

"Yes," said Ammonius. "And we were successful."

"What?" I said. "That's impossible."

"You do not know your history," said Ammonius. "Six

hundred years ago we overthrew the Kings, and a Priest of Ammon took the throne, and the city of Thebes was ruled by the Order of the Priests from that time forward."

"No," I said. "No, this cannot be true."

"You are a Northerner," said Ammonius, "so you do not know. The story in the North was that a dynasty of Libyan Kings was ruling. But there was a tacit agreement not to interfere with the theocracy in the South, and in both Upper and Lower Egypt, whoever was nominally the ruler, it was Ammon who ruled over all."

"So ever since the invasion of the Hyksos was repelled," I said, trying to take it all in, "the Priests of Ammon were plotting to overthrow the throne."

"Basically," said Ammonius. "With the army, we thought it was the only way possible to save Egypt from outside invasion. We may not have been wrong. But the records tell of pestilence and invasion spreading to all lands in the end, with the fall of Caphtor. Egypt alone was the only one able to repel the chaos. Due to our efforts."

"This is what you meant," I said, "when you said that we Northerners did not know the lengths you had gone to. But tell me, what was this power struggle between the Kings, and the Order of Ammon?"

"You have heard of King Tutmose III?" said Ammonius.

"Yes," I said. "He built great temples."

"You will not have heard of his Aunt. Her name has

been struck from the records. Why? She opposed the Order."

"His Aunt?" I said.

"Yes, she was a Female King, as has happened from time to time in our history. Now you could not say that she was some kind of valiant defender of truth. She poisoned her husband, because he caught her having an affair with the general, and usurped the throne from him, and from her nephew, whose throne it was by right."

"She does not sound like a good person," I said.

"She was not," said Ammonius. "She was horrible, an absolutely horrible tyrant, and that is what the power struggle was all about. Try to understand: yes, my Order was allied with the army, and implicitly with the worship of Set. Set is, as you know, not entirely evil. Yet we were not trying to destroy Egypt, we were trying to save it from its decadence. These Kings were not like in the Old Days. They had lost their right to rule. The Royal Throne was collapsing, and they did terrible things."

"It sounds like," I said. "Neither side was on the side of justice."

Ammonius stopped. He had been speaking to me with a passionate intensity. Now, his shoulders slumped. "Perhaps it is true," he said at last. "And my Order, the Priesthood of Ammon, has presided over the destruction of all that we hold dear. Now we see Egypt ruled by foreigners, and our holy religion perverted. But we were poor guardians. More than a thousand years ago, when these events I am relating to you occurred, we were unable to keep the cohesion of our society."

"Tell me about the Heretic King," I said.

"He was the last gasp," said Ammonius. "The last attempt of the Royal Throne to regain the powers it had before the Hyksos invasion. The Jews think that he was a radical, a revolutionary who sought to usher in a new kind of divine worship. Nothing could be further from the truth. All of the breaks he made in the tradition of our art were an attempt to return to the times of absolute rule. Everything he did was an effort to save the throne. And it backfired.

"He was a tyrant, and he banned the Priesthood of Ammon entirely. That was his real aim for banning all other gods, and he targeted our Order specifically. He created a secret police, which reported on anyone worshiping a God that was not directly controlled by him. They ransacked the old monuments. And of course, because he was opposed to our faction, the faction of the Army and the Priests, he neglected the Empire entirely. This was reactionary: he wanted to return to the time of the distant past, like the time of Imhotep, when the King was a God and none could oppose him."

Ammonius was silent, staring off into space. "Then Ramesses came," I prompted.

"Yes of course," said Ammonius. "The downfall of the Heretic was chaos, because of his tyranny. There was no sense in which he loved justice. Nor did he have any new spiritual truth. It is the center of our religion, as you know, that all Gods are one. So proclaiming only one God can only be a way to control others, and to pit one order against another. In the fallout the Army took over."

"That was the end of anyone seriously opposing the Order of Ammon. All those great monuments that Seti I, and his son Ramesses made, these were all attempts to cover up the fact that they were figureheads. They were army generals who had appropriated the divine throne at the behest of the Order of Ammon. We held all the strings."

"I never knew any of this," I said.

"That is because it is not spoken of," said Ammonius. "Except in the Temple of Thoth."

"And Amenhotep, son of Hapu?"

"He advised the father of the Heretic. You see, even in those horrible times, there was one who came who had the light of Imhotep. He was a scribe, but he was far-seeing enough to understand the Old Ways. He designed the great temples, like the Temple of Karnak. Without his guidance, there is no way we could have survived the calamity of the Heretic. That is why we honor his memory, and we do not speak the name of that evil King."

"The brother of Imhotep," I said. "At the twilight of our age."

"You could say," said Ammonius, "that Imhotep was the sage who began Egyptian culture. Amenhotep son of

Hapu was the sage responsible for bringing it to its conclusion. Yes, there were people afterwards, who walked and talked like they were Egyptians, and who built monuments like Egyptians, even worshiped the same Gods as the Egyptians. But after this, our culture was never quite the same."

I found Bentreshyt in the garden of the Temple, weeding the base of the geraniums. "You are learning much," she said to me. "You are becoming wise."

"I am thinking," I said. "That I will pledge myself to Imhotep."

"You already are pledged to Imhotep, Kaires. Or rather, Imhotep is pledged to you."

"I know," I said. "I have seen the *akh* of Imhotep. Or the *akh* of one of his servants."

"You are favored," she said. She paused, and then continued weeding the geraniums. "Kaires is not your real name."

"How do you know?" I said.

"I am like Isis," she said. "I know the secret names of all things."

"Well, you're not going to get mine."

"I am pledged to the Goddess Seshat, Kaires," said

Bentreshyt. "I do not eat fish. I do not make love. I do not even eat bread on a holy day. You know, I have not had a drop of water this whole day, and I am here in the fire of the Sun, tending to this garden." She bent down, and I could see the black Earth clinging to her arms and fingers, yet somehow making them even more beautiful in the translucent light.

"You are not just pledged to Seshat," I said. "The truth is, Bentreshyt, that you are pledged to the Goddess Renpetneferet."

She looked up at me, and smiled. For the first time, it reached her eyes. "Ah," she said. "Now I see the boy knows *my* name."

"If Imhotep is the start of our philosophy," I said to Ammonius, "and Amenhotep son of Hapu is the end of it, then what would you say our philosophy is?"

"Oh," said Ammonius. "The Books of Wisdom. What else would philosophy be?"

"I suppose that's true," I said.

"Is not the initiate in the training book, *The Chamber of Darkness,* 'The One Who Loves Wisdom?' This is what we teach."

"Who are our chief philosophers then?"

"You sound like a Greek," said Ammonius. "The only philosopher who matters is Thoth. What can personal wisdom be, next to the divine?"

"But if you had to make a list, who would you say?"

"Well," said Ammonius, "of everyone who has written an *Instruction,* the first was Imhotep. Then came Hardjedef, who was a son of King Khufu, the King of the

Great Pyramid. Then there was Ptahhotep, who like Imhotep was a vizier. His son was Akhethotep, to whom his instruction is addressed. Then there was Kaires, your namesake, who was the father Kagemni, who wrote the *Instruction of Kagemni*."

"Imhotep, Hardjedef, Ptahhotep," I said. "Akhethotep, Kaires, Kagemni."

"Then we have the reign of King Amenemhat I," said Ammonius. "This was after the rebellion of the *reshyt*, which Imhotep warned of in his *Instruction*, but which became inevitable after the reign of Pepi II. During this rebellion, there was Khety, who wrote an instruction. These were the philosophers who, because they had witnessed most the breaches of justice in their times, championed the ancient alliance of Justice and Truth: Neferty, Ptahmedjehuty, Khakheperraseneb.

"These are the greatest of our philosophers."

"But Father," I said. "What is this book which Imhotep wrote?"

"It is a book for how to live well," said Ammonius. "And a reminder to the King's Court, which almost did not receive him."

"The famine..." I said.

"Yes, there was a famine in the time of Imhotep," said Ammonius. "Caused by the negligence and disorder of the nobility."

"This is what he was warning us about," I said.

"Yes," said Ammonius. "This is why I say Imhotep began our philosophy; Amenhotep ended it."

"Because of your Order," I said. "Tell me, what do our philosophers say regarding the soul, and the parts of the soul?"

"There are five parts of the soul," said Ammonius. "The Ba. The Ka. The Name. The Shadow. The Akh."

"Is there not also the Heart, and the Physical Body?"

"Yes," said Ammonius. "But the Ba contains the body, and the body contains the heart."

"What is the relationship between the Ba and the Ka?"

"The Ka transmigrates," said Ammonius. "The Ba abides."

"Can you explain this more to me, Father?"

"The Ba is the personality. It contains the set of all that one ever is, was, and shall be, as it occurs in Eternity. Thus the Ba is what attends in the Land of the Dead; it is the Ba which returns to inhabit the image of a person, or the embalmed body. This is the way in which the Ba is connected with the Name, or the representation."

"So is the Name the Ba, Father?"

"No. The Name represents the Ba, and by saying the name, or making an offering, one invokes a Ba."

"I still do not understand what you mean Father, when you say the Ba is an image of Eternity."

"The World of the Dead is timeless," said Ammonius.

"We have within it the true Forms of all that we see here before us now. In that realm all our actions are complete. There you exist as a Ba, in the fullness of your actions, either good, or bad. This is the true meaning of the Weighing of the Heart. The Weighing of the Heart is happening all the time."

"But how does the Ka relate, Father?"

"The Ka is the breath of life. It is the vital force. It is the cause of life. When life is done, the Ka departs and goes somewhere else. It does not abide as the Ba does. Yet when you make an offering before the shrine of one who is dead, it is to the Ka that you make the offering, although it is the Ba which arrives, and inhabits the statue or the Name."

"Why is this, Father?"

"You are approaching the heart of the mystery of re-incarnation, my son."

"Then what is the Shadow?"

"The Shadow is the opposite of every Name, and every Ba, and is a necessary part of its existence. Even now, you have a shadow from your very body, which is the incar-nation of your Ba. But you do not know it, so you do not know your Name. This is the meaning of the saying 'Keep your shadow close.' "

"Oh Father," I said. "I understand the relationship between the Ka and the Ba, and the relationship between the Shadow and the Name, but tell me, how do the Ka and the Ba combine to form the Akh?"

225

"This is the purpose, my son, of all our philosophy. All of the men whom I have listed made this their goal. Some, such as Imhotep and Amenhotep, have achieved it. For if one can achieve sainthood within one's lifetime, then the Ba and the Ka will unite after death and form the Akh. Then immortality will be achieved."

"But what of those," I said, "to whom we leave offerings, and yet they were not saints or sages in their lives?"

"For those who do not attain union with God, we keep to the old rites such that their Bas might still have a chance of achieving salvation through their descendants. This is why the saddest thing is a lineage that has died out, for it traps the Ba-souls forever in the Land of the Dead, with no one to speak for them."

"What a terrible fate," I cried, "for those who are left in the Land of the Dead, with no one to remember them."

"Yes my son," said Ammonius. "But remember, that the soul also transmigrates, and that when the Ka completes its journey within the cycles of time, then also those Ba-souls will be released. So there is no tragedy that lasts forever."

"This must be true, oh Father," I said, "For the Kas and the Bas of the common people, but what of the soul of the King?"

"You are now speaking of the religion of Osiris," said Ammonius. "This was the religion founded by Menes. It was different than the religion founded by Imhotep, and was the religion of the masses, whereas Imhotep's religion is the religion of the educated. This is why it is said the Egyptians have two religions."

"But what is taught in the religion of Osiris, for I desire to know that too."

"You remember what I said to you last time?" said Ammonius. "Concerning the Order of my God, and the conflict for the throne?"

"Yes Father," I said.

"That was a conflict between these two religions.

"The religion of Menes was centered in Abydos. The religion of Imhotep was centered in Memphis. The way of Osiris was a way for the masses to attain salvation in the person of the Divine Kingship. The King embodied the Holy Word which completes creation. As an incarnation of the ultimate upon Earth, he also wielded absolute power. As the Osirian way fell into decadence, and the later Kings were not able to embody this principle - as Imhotep warned us about - the collapse represented by the Heretic was inevitable."

"So you are saying," I said, "that the religion of Imhotep is the true religion of Egypt."

"It is the tradition," said Ammonius, "that has steered Egypt, that has been the rudder of the sacred barque, in the same way that Thoth, allied with the Moon, keeps the ledger of the sacred accounts for Re. And keeps the Sun turning in its course in the sky."

"What are these spells, Father, which keep the Sun turning in the sky?"

"Oh, my son," said Ammonius. "You must know we are in great danger. Across Egypt, the Oracles of the Gods are becoming silent. The divine waters are dying up. The Gods no longer speak to man. They are withdrawing from the world. We are in a crisis. Fools think that the Sun will keep turning across the sky without our ritual aid, but they do not realize that just as there are two religions, there are two Suns."

"Two Suns, Father?"

"Yes, my Son. One appears to be the Sun we see there, which looks as though it revolves around us every day, rising in the East and setting in the West. The other is the Central Fire, the Flame Imperishable, about which the other Sun turns, as indeed our Earth does too, and all the planets with it. Now if we do not tend to the Sun of appearances with our prayers, and our constant adoration, it will cease to go across the sky. Then, no matter how it may appear, that there is still a fire in the sky, in our hearts it will be darkness, for the God of the Sun will have no way to speak to mankind, and we will be rudderless."

"In that era, my Son, which is coming, there will be no word of the Gods anymore. Men will regard the Divine as something laughable, a fantasy. They will not be able to see what is right in front of their eyes: that the world is sacred, and deserves honor, praise and worship in the mystery of its being. They will cut themselves off from the Divine and, like children, they will cease to believe in God. Then will demons come, and drive them to madness, and chaos will rule their world. Yet still they will not realize what is happening to them: they will blame other demons, and cease to be aware that the cause of their distress are the Gods who, in their arrogance and naivete, they had banished from the world.

"Then will the stars not keep to their course. The seas will rise, and fire will rain upon the world. It is only in that time that perhaps salvation will come. In that time, I foretell, will be the true end of Our Philosophy, and we will know whether the work of Egypt has been for good, or ill."

"Father," I said, "thank you for the lesson."

I went to the House of Life to find the *Instruction of Imhotep.* There were many Books of Thoth in the House of Life at the Temple Library of Khemenu. And there were many there that had been written by Imhotep, or that our tradition had ascribed to Imhotep: books of medicine and gynecology, books of spells, and incantations. There were stories about his deeds, and stories about the magic of his akh. It took me a long time before I found the Book that I was looking for, the philosophical book, the book of his Instruction.

THE INSTRUCTION OF IMHOTEP

The Governor of the City, the vizier, Imhotep, he said: "It is now the Sunset of my life. I feel old age descend upon me. My bones do not bend. I am become feeble. Again I fall into the state of a child. What was good in the morning of my life turns to evil in the evening. The eyes are small; the ears are deaf. My wife has died, she has left me, and I am alone. My daughters are now God's Wives in the Temple. I am alone, and what can there be for me left to do?

My old lord, King Netjerikhet, he has gone to the next world. His son, the Divine Sekhemkhet rules, and I lack the strength to complete his monument.

Therefore, my servant, I command you to take my words to the place of my children, that they and their descendants, all the children of Egypt, might not forget the sacrifice of the forefathers: that they can carry their good name forward, that they will not go astray."

Said the Majesty of this God: "Instruct them, then, in the words of old time; may they be a wonder unto the children of princes, that they may enter and hearken with him. Make straight all their hearts; and discourse with them, without causing weariness."

He said unto his children:

"1. Say what you mean. Do not contradict the heart. For the one whose speech is true has beneficence, he engenders justice: his heart is not crooked.

2. It may seem that those who speak Falsehood prosper, while those of the Truth suffer. This is not so. All ill word and deed twist the heart: they will suffer, they cannot persist in Falsehood for long.

3. Let not thy speech contradict thine actions. For it is the greatest wounding of the heart to persist in Falsehood, it destroys the soul, and cripples the holy Word.

4. Actions and Words are the two thoughts of God. They are the means God has given to Man for the construction of his kingdom. Use them well.

5. Speaking is a privilege, not a right. If you misuse this Word that God has given you: behold, your posture will become stooped, your continence like the continence of beasts.

6. The existence of Words and Deeds confer respon-

sibilities upon Man, not privileges. Man is responsible to his brethren, the beings of God's temple of Land, Sea, and Sky.

7. Speak the holy Names well. Know that what you are naming is the heart of God, and that by this you sing to all Creation.

8. But to he who speaks a Name in Falsehood, in contradiction of Word and Deed, to him will his heart go to the devourer, he will not return.

9. If you are in the Temple, and you are conducting the holy offerings, know that your actions are watched, they are not yours alone.

10. If you think that there is space for insincerity of conduct in ritual, think again. If you treat ritual like a game, you are not fit for it.

11. If you go before your Lord, be obedient. Do not disobey authority without cause. To do so sows ruination in the Mind of God.

12. If you are aware that someone higher than you has done a misdeed, choose carefully where you want to speak out. If you can, go through your Lord and do it in public.

13. Secrecy breeds secrecy, envy breeds disgrace. Therefore my children, speak your heart truly before the Tribunal of God.

14. If you are in the presence of a noble, and that one disrespects you, be noble of conduct in return. It will remind that one what his station truly is.

15. If your actions inspire envy in the hearts of others, be lighthearted, be humble. Do not react. In this way they will see you are sincere.

16. Sincerity is the greatest gift God has given to Man. It is the candle of Truth, and therefore, of Justice.

17. If you are in court and a great crime is done, while everyone else is whispering "what shall we do?" Keep the heart steady, and do not be bowed by honor or disgrace.

18. The paths of life are like sharp rocks. It is Truth which allows you to navigate your boat to the other side. The heart is your rudder, Truth your steering arm.

19. If Falsehood previals, and men speak against you, it is not ignominious to retire. Falsehood eats falsehood;

soon Truth will come to light, and people will say, 'Where did he go?'

20. As it is for a child to a parent, one must submit entirely to their will. These are the ones who have clothed you, they have given you life, how can you speak against them?

21. Piety is for a child to take care of their elders. It is for that child not to go away while they grow old.

22. What good are you if you do not care for your elders? Truly, I say, the one who does not take care of his parents is no better than a beast.

23. For the time of old age is lowly, one becomes stooped again like a child, and feebleminded. Therefore, take care of the ones who once gave you everything, return like with like.

24. To contradict a teacher or an elder is a grave sin. Respect the ones who are older than you. You do not know what they have seen, what they have witnessed.

25. What is given in youth is taken in old age. Oh, that I could have the wisdom of old age in youth! Therefore listen to your elders: they are trying to help you.

26. Be good to your wife. Do not treat her like chattel. She is the one upon whom the household lives or dies.

27. Be good to your husband. Do not hem him in like a bird. He is the one upon whom the household lives or dies.

28. If there is Truth between husband and wife, the order of the family will be good. If there is not Truth between husband and wife, the bonds of blood will be broken, and the household will weep.

29. If there is strife among siblings, who shall be the decider, but the Father? If there is strife among nations, who shall be the decider, but the King?

30. Therefore be loyal to the courts, and do not contradict them. The rule of law is the cornerstone of Justice, it keeps men in harmony with God.

31. Be kind to those who are destitute, and give of your property to them. Do not turn them away, treat them as your guests.

32. When there is famine do not turn up your nose and say, 'Well I have plenty to eat.' For you do not know

when you yourself will next be hungry.

33. When there is famine, remember that your neighbors are your brothers and sisters. How can this depend on social rank?

34. Oh children, I tell you that service is the greatest designator of worth. Therefore let not those who are high say to those who are low, 'you owe me.'

35. Therefore, in times of famine, it is the duty of those who have much to give to those who have little. Then they show their worth, and their rank is secured.

36. But to those who transgress this, and treat rank as something to be coveted: that one invites revolution. His house will be torn down, and stones thrown upon him.

37. Do not be an office-seeker. Do not throw yourself away after rank. Guard the heart, speak truly, and let your actions be their own reward.

38. The balance of the heart is achieved when Words and Deeds are in harmony.

39. Therefore do not turn away from the Word of God, nor this Word that I have given you. Stay true to the

whole of Creation, and do not lose sight of the work of God.

40. For this lifetime is short, and passes in the blink of an eye. But God is eternal, and everlasting. Practice these words, that your return to him might be happy.

IT IS FINISHED

FROM ITS BEGINNING TO ITS END

EVEN AS FOUND IN WRITING.

"Father," I said. "Last we spoke you told me of a time that will come when men will lose touch with the world of the Gods. How, then, can our religion survive?"

"My child," said Ammonius. "You speak of a sad thing. For in the time that is coming men will lose sight of the world of the Gods. They will think that it is a fiction, because they will transgress in their speech, and they will become feebleminded, like children. Then they will think that they know everything, when in fact they know nothing.

"But all hope is not lost, my son. If one God survives, let us say, for the sake of argument, that Thoth survives - if just Thoth survives, then the heart of our religion has survived."

"How can this be so, Father, if all the other Gods have died?"

"I will tell you," he said. "There is the Name of God,

and there is the Image of God. Even if the Name is translated, and the Image transforms, even if the God's name is spoken in the language of a foreigner, then that God will have survived. As long as there is an unbroken line of descent between Master and pupil, the God will survive. Even now, between us and Imhotep, there are more than two thousand years. Even if more than two thousand years pass between now and this time in the future, if there is a lineage, what is there to fear?"

"But if the rest of our religion is gone, Father, what is the use?"

"Do you remember what I told you last time? The religion of Thoth is the rudder which steers the ship of the Gods. It keeps the Sun turning in the sky. If all other parts of the religion died, but this one survived, it would be enough to say Egypt has survived.

"Let us say, for the sake of argument, that in order to hide the God from the foreigners, we are to place the God within a small glass jar. This jar will be a perfect sphere, like the cosmos and the encircling World Serpent. Now, even though the Sun has stopped going across the sky, because the rites are stopped - and here I mean, the God, the Image of the Sun has stopped going across the sky, although it will appear to men that there is still a Sun, they will not be in harmony with it. Even though the Sun has stopped going across the sky, we can hide the Sun in this glass jar, let's say, and disguise it as a series of chemical operations."

"Yes Father?"

"In this way, let us say, the religion of Thoth is preserved — whose true wisdom, as you know, is not contained in any book, but consists in the power of *singing the world into being.* This means offering praise and thanksgiving to the forms of God which confront us as stars and planets, as birds and beasts, and as elements. For in speaking their holy names they are given a house in eternity, and we fulfill the service that God intended us for.

"Then, at a time in the far future, when the time is right, this chemical jar will crack, and splinter into many fragments. In that time will be the era when the Sun must be put back in the sky. Although this may take a few centuries."

"How, Father, are we to put the Sun in the sky if the myth has fragmented?"

He held up his hand to me. "Do you see this hand? Do you see these five fingers? These five fingers are the sciences. But all sciences come from Thoth. Five fingers, one hand. Therefore, reunite the sciences, and the Wisdom of Thoth will live again."

"Then Father, please, tell me the secret, I must know: how do you make a dead God live again?"

Ammonius sighed. "The secret you are talking about is contained in the relation between the Ogdoad and the Ennead. You cannot make a God live again, for the Gods are ever living. Yet, the image of a God can die, which is a great tragedy for Man, but not for God. My son, do you know what the Ogdoad is?"

"These are the 8 Gods of Infinity, in whose city we reside."

"Yes. And these 8 Infinites exist before time. Therefore, they cannot be created or destroyed. Therefore, no matter what happens in the world of man, the Ogdoad will always exist, and will always influence the Mind of man, whether he is aware of it or no."

"What of the Ennead, Father?"

"The Ennead and the World-Serpent are one, as you yourself have seen. The Ennead are the Gods of Re, and they are the Gods which escort and secure the path of the Sun. Yet they are kept in their path by Thoth, who holds the true wisdom, and harmonizes them with the Ogdoad. In this way we can say that what is Inside reflects what is Outside, that the Sun goes across the sky, and the myth is in harmony with eternity. This is the secret of the Ogdoad and the Ennead."

"Then the 8 Infinites themselves create the Gods, Father?"

"Yes my son, and if the image of just a single God has survived, this God, working with the Ogdoad, could put the Sun back in the sky, providing that those who entreated this God had a sufficient understanding of the true meaning of these rites."

"What then is the World Serpent, Father?"

"It is the Ennead, and a form of Eternity. It is the Time which continuously recreates itself, the time of transmigration. For this reason, the Ogdoad carry with them the Shen ring, the image of eternity, and it is this ring which we write around a Name to protect it, and to ensure its divine status."

"What is the other form of Time, Father?"

"It is the arrow, the line which strikes Eternity like the eye of the Uraeus. It is the palm fronds which the Ogdoad carry, signifying the Unit of a Year, and it is this palm frond which Seshat inscribes the divine hall of records into at the will of Thoth, for she is his partner. And also, this form of Time is the meaning of the Name of Renpetneferet."

"How are we to balance these two forms of Time, Father?"

"In the same way that Imhotep teaches, my son," said Ammonius. "By balancing the heart, and balancing Word and Deed, we balance these two forms of time. This is the true meaning of the Weighing of the Heart. The soul both transmigrates, and it abides. That is why it is such a loss when a Ba is fed to the devourer."

"Although in the end their salvation is secured."

"Depending on the perspective of man, or the perspective of God. But the nature of God is Goodness."

"Father," I said. "Thank you for the lesson."

One day I came upon a strange machine in one of the chapels off the temple of Thoth. It was made out of cedar planks, like the Cedars of Byblos, and seemed to consist of two levers turned upside down. There were a number of split cedar logs sitting beside it, and it was about two times the size of my body.

"Bentreshyt," I said as she was passing, "what is this machine?"

"Oh, this?" she said. "This is the machine that was used to put the facing stones upon the pyramids."

"But," I said, "I was trying to invent a machine like this. It would be a new kind of shaduf."

"Were you?" she said. "Isn't that something? Well, it turns out that your ancestors have already invented this machine long ago."

"It is like," I said, fingering the levers, "someone turned a balance scale upside-down."

"Hmm," said Bentreshyt. "I had never thought of that before. You see you load a stone in here, and the stone can be quite large, and then you winch it up using the double levers - two men - and helpers pile the logs underneath to raise it up. It makes bringing the stones up to the top of the pyramid child's play."

"And the raising of every stone is the Weighing of the Heart," I said.

Bentreshyt laughed. "That's very poetic," she said. "Where are you getting all of these ideas from, your conversations with Ammonius?"

"Yes," I said. "You know, he is even teaching me the secrets of Renpetneferet."

Bentreshyt shook her head. "Ammonius does not know the secrets of Renpetneferet. There are secrets the women kept even from the men."

"Then will you tell me?" I asked.

She paused, looking down at her hands. "You are very brave," she said at last. "But like all men you will meet a bad end."

"What does that mean?" I said, thinking she was joking.

"You know Renpetneferet was once the chief of the attendants of the Royal Wives. She was in charge of all the female maidservants."

"Like Sinuhe," I said.

"No," she said. "Sinuhe was in charge of the men.

Renpetneferet was in charge of the women. There is a difference."

"So she was a maidservant," I said.

"The greatest maidservant and God's Wife to Bast. But she spent so much time with the Royal Wives that King Djoser started to desire her. He wanted her for himself. He kidnapped her, and Imhotep had to rescue her. It caused a scandal."

"Did it?" I said.

"Yes," said Bentreshyt, "and then the Assyrians saw that our country was weak, and tried to invade. King Djoser was in the field, and the only way that Imhotep could save his wife - who had been faithful, she had fooled the King and not slept with him - was if he dueled an Assyrian magician in a combat of spells."

"And did he? Did he win?"

"Well," said Bentreshyt. "Egypt is still here. For now."

"You know many stories, Bentreshyt," I said.

"Yes," she said. "And you have much wisdom. But you do not follow it."

"How so?" I said.

"If you had followed your wisdom you would have told me your real name from the start. Then I could have protected you."

The floor fell out from under my feet. "Then..."

"I know you are the fugitive. You cannot hide it from me. I know the secret names of all things."

She gathered a few scraps of leather from a side table, and made to go outside to tend to her trees.

"Wait," I said. "Bentreshyt."

She paused, and looked at me. "What?"

"You will not tell, will you?"

"God, what do you take me for? I do not love the Greeks."

"Only I am so grateful to be here."

"You are a wayward vagabond," she said, "who has little love for the Gods except what they can do for him. I see that now."

"No," I said. "That is not true. I love Thoth, and I love our religion. I will die defending it."

"If that is true," she said, "then where are your parents?"

"My father is dead," I said. "And my mother is still in Sais."

"Because you have gone storming across the world looking for secret knowledge and you have left no one to take care of her."

"That is not true," I said.

"It is," she said. "And everything you have learned here you could have gained in Sais if you had only paid attention to what God was offering you. Instead you have crashed halfway around the world because you are a malcontent and a nincompoop."

"Why are you saying these things?" I said.

"Because —" she said, and stopped. She picked up the leather and stepped out the door. "I have work to do."

"Father," I said. "What can you tell me about Atlantis, which the Greek poet Solon says he learned of from our records?"

"Ah," said Ammonius. "Yes, this Atlantis was a real place, but it is not quite the way Plato describes it. The truth is, Atlantis and the island of Caphtor are one."

"Caphtor?" I said.

"Yes," said Ammonius, "the island in the Aegean. We traded with these people from the Northern Sea for many generations. It is true that they were very civilized. They roofed their temples with orichalcum, and their palaces had pipes of hot and cold running water. They practiced a religion of the Double-Axe, and they worshiped the Bull as their sacred animal. Then their island was destroyed in a cataclysm of fire and water."

"Was this island larger than Libya and Asia combined? And did it sink into the Sea?"

"What? No, Caphtor is not that big. And it is still there. But their palaces were destroyed by a great wave. Then they were invaded by the Greeks, and that began a period of decline. As their society crumbled, the Peoples of the Sea - refugees from the destruction of Caphtor - made war against Egypt, Greece, and Babylon. Incidentally, this is also the time when the Trojan War occurred, and that is the period in history the Greek tales are based on."

"Ah," I said. "Then the destruction of Atlantis does not have great antiquity."

"No, my son," said Ammonius. "It happened only about a thousand years ago. But we have these records, whereas the Babylonians do not, because alone of the great nations of the world Egypt stood against the foreigners. King Ramesses III defeated the Sea Peoples and enslaved them. They did not trouble Egypt again."

"So this is what is meant in Solon's poem, when he speaks of the war against Egypt and Greece?"

"Precisely, my son," said Ammonius. "It is this era."

It was night, and I found Bentreshyt standing by the retaining wall, looking out over a reservoir of water.

"Leave," she said. "I cannot speak to you."

"Bentreshyt," I said. "Listen."

"What is your actual name?" she said. "Tell me."

"Psammethicus," I said. "But my friends call me Psa."

"I knew it," she said. "You are not a Kaires. You are much more like a Saiite King than an ancient sage."

"What does that mean?" I said.

"It means you are decadent." She threw a leaf into the water.

"Bentreshyt," I said. "Why have you pledged yourself to Renpetneferet?"

She turned, and met my gaze. The moon was lighting up her eyes like deep wells. "Because my Akh is calling to me."

"Your akh?" I said.

251

She nodded. "Yes, my akh is calling to me at the end of the world."

"At the end of the world?" I said, smiling. "And where would that be?"

"Not where, Psa-Kaires. When."

"But this world is eternal," I said. "It cannot be created or destroyed."

"Oh my dear, dear Psammetichus," she said, and I saw tears in her eyes, "when are you going to understand that there are two forms of Time?"

Then I knew. In the silent moonlit garden of the Temple of Thoth, I felt my akh call to me, singing to me from the end of Time. "We have known each other before," I said.

"Yes," Bentreshyt nodded.

"And we are here now," I said. "But Bentreshyt —"

"Do not say it," she said. "I am pledged to the Goddess Seshat, and it is my duty to remain pure. If I break my vow, I must commit ritual suicide. Do you not understand? Ammonius will force me to."

"But my heart, Bentreshyt, my heart is calling out to you."

"Imhotep," she said. "We will be together again, before the end of the circles of time."

"But I am not Imhotep," I said. "I cannot be Imhotep."

"Then," she said, smiling sadly, "Maybe your akh is

one of his helpers."

"Who does that make you then?"

"Me?" she said. "I will remain chief of the Ladies-In-Waiting forever, even when there are not any Ladies left to wait on, and my Name becomes crushed in the dust of Time."

"Renpetneferet is with you," I said. "I see her in you. Renpetneferet is with you even now."

She turned to me, and I saw the Goddess within her. The Goddess spoke through her, and delivered the *Lamentation of Renpetneferet*. I heard these words, and learned the true secrets of the pyramids. I am a poor witness to these words, but I heard them. Even now, my akh, helper of Imhotep, carries them with me.

"Psammetichus," said Bentreshyt. "My heart has never felt this way before. What does it mean?"

"It means, love," I said. "That our souls are bound together more closely than the weft and warp of the fabric of time."

"But what if I fail?" she said. "What if I am impure, and my ba is fed to the devourer? Bentreshyt will go forever into dust, and all the goodness of Egypt will fall. Men will forget it, and Falsehood will descend like darkness upon the world."

"But your akh," I said. "Your akh will remain. And my akh will too. I will find you again, and we will make holiday together, in memory of the old times, even when everyone else has forgotten."

"I do not want to see Egypt that way," she said. "As bones and corpses, just the skeletons of monuments. And scavengers picking over the bones, looking for scraps of magic."

"My love," I said. "Think not of Egypt. Think of the Gods Egypt was made for. Eternity is there." I touched her cheek, and it was soft. A tear from her eyes caught on her lashes, and it mirrored the Moon. I brought my face close to her, I touched my brow against hers.

"Don't," she said, "Don't do it. Or my ba will die."

"You cannot remain here," said Ammonius. "You have tempted Bentreshyt."

"But Father," I said. "We did not break any vows."

"Nevertheless," said Ammonius. "Your presence here is a temptation to her. You will draw her away from her service, and she will live in sin. You cannot behave this way if you want to serve the Gods."

"I have self control," I protested.

"You do not!" Ammonius slammed his hand upon the table again. "Have you listened to nothing I told you? You Northerners are all the same. What you say in Word, you do not practice in Deed, and this is the decadence that has always ruled the Delta. Begone from here! I want you out of this Temple by nightfall, or I will call the Castle Guards."

"Father —"

"Do not tempt me boy!"

I paused. Bowed, and turned to go. "Thank you for

the lesson," I said.

I gathered my belongings: the letter, and my cubes of incense. I left the Temple of Thoth, and exited Khemenu under cover of darkness through the Gate of the Moon. I went through the desert, and lived like a Sand-farer. No man saw me. I was invisible.

I let my name be forgotten.

EPILOGUE

Saqqara

I gave the ferryman a drachma, and stepped on his reed boat. It was afternoon, and the Sun was setting across White-Walled Memphis. The shadows from the columns and the obelisks were lengthening. Smoke was on the wind. Criers were advertising their wares to laborers coming from the fields. It was the harvest season.

"Thank you, sir," said the ferryman. "Where can I take you?"

"Take me to the road that leads to the City of the Dead," I said. He put an oar in the water, and began rowing across the river.

I had tried to take a side. But I had been prosecuted by the Greeks, and expelled from the Temple of my countrymen. I was caught between two forms of Time, drawn and quartered, and they were tearing me in half. Duplicitous, that's me. Stuck in the middle.

The ferryman dropped me off at the other side of the river, and I set out over the hills to reach the necropolis of the Kings, in the Red Desert. I stopped at the top of a hill, and rested. The Sun was nearing the Horizon. I took my father's letter from my bag, and read it again.

My son,

It warms the heart of a man in old age to hear that you are going to get an education among the Greeks. Death nears me. What was good in the morning has become evil in the evening. My bones are weak. My eyes and my ears are small.

I am grateful to the Priest Manetho for all the guidance he has given you at that school. Unlike the great teachers of old, I do not have any Instruction for you, for I have a son who I already know will do great things.

All I will say is this: I am so very, very proud of you, my son. Good luck in the city of the Greeks, and may you do our culture proud, represent it well, and teach those Greeks what a true Egyptian is capable of.

Your loving father,
Kaires

I set down the letter and wept. Then I stood, and

looked over the crest. The Sun was going down between two hills. I raised my hands, and silently offered him praise. *To you, Oh Lord, greatest Lord, in the image of the Most High, I offer my life.* Then I continued on over the hills, a silent pilgrim on an endless quest.

It was twilight when I reached the Necropolis of King Djoser. There was a crowd of men out in front of the doors, but I ignored them, and entered through the triple gates, coming into the sanctuary. The cult was busy. Shrines and market stalls had been set up throughout the enclosure. People were selling their goods, and the air was thick with incense from so many making offerings to the Gods. I wandered through the reliefs showing the visions of Djoser's Eternal Sed Festival, pondering the carvings and trying to glean what wisdom I could from the glyphs.

There were two forms of Time. There was a rift in History. And I was caught between it.

"Hello, sir," said a hawker. "Would you like to make an offering to Imhouthes?"

"What?" I said. "Imhotep?"

"Yes," said the hawker. "I have them right here." He gestured to a blanket, where he had laid out about twenty mummified Ibis birds.

"Let me get this straight," I said, horrified. "You have these, for *sale?*"

"Yes, of course," said the hawker. "So that anyone, even a tourist like you, can make an offering."

"I am not a tourist and that is sacrilege," I said. "You are supposed to make a sacrifice. A mummified creature is not something you can just buy in a box."

"What are you getting on about?" said the hawker. "It's a new era. Everyone can make an offering to Imhouthes now."

"How do I even know that these are even real?" I said. "How do I know you have recited the proper spells?" I hit one of the birds, and its beak fell off. It had been glued on, and whatever it was was hardly mummified.

"Hey!" shouted the hawker. "This man is messing with my wares!"

"You are selling sacrificial offerings under false pretenses. This is an insult to yourself, and to the God!"

A small commotion was forming, a crowd was gathering.

"He is a thief!" shouted the hawker. "He has come here to tamper with my wares."

"How dare you insult this Prophet, who initiated our traditions, who built this great monument, and ask me to pay for a sacrifice to him that is not even real?"

One of the temple guards pushed his way through the crowd. "What seems to the problem here?" the guard said in Greek.

"This man is selling fake offerings," I said.

"He has tampered with my wares," said the hawker.

"You should not do that," the guard said to me,

"whether his offerings were fake or real. All are allowed to sell their wares here, whether they are true or false. It is the responsibility of the customer to discern this."

"But," I said. "This is a temple..."

"I am sorry," said the guard. "I am going to have to escort you from the premises now."

He led me outside of the complex, and pushed me out the gate. "If I see you again, I will arrest you."

I stepped outside, broken. Expelled from every temple. The Moon was rising over the tombs of Saqqara. How was I to make my living? How was I to fulfill the purpose of my akh, if everywhere I went I was met with disdain? Of what possible service could I be to Imhotep?

Then I heard the crowd of men that I had ignored before, standing outside the gate and chattering excitedly. They were Greek tourists.

"So this colossus," one of them was saying, "which they say is Memnon the Ethiopian who fought in the Trojan War. It speaks, brothers, I swear it! It whispers mysterious magical words of the Egyptians, secret teachings that, if the initiate learns them, will give them the key to the whole of the universe!"

"The whole of the universe?" said another.

"Riches!" said the first. "Love! Magic, all of this and more — for the Egyptians keep many secrets."

"I should like to be initiated," said a third, "into these secrets. Who would I have to pay to be let into one of their temples?"

"No," said the first, "they do not let foreigners into their temples. They keep their secrets locked close. But they say that a New Age is dawning, the Age of Pisces, and in this era the Egyptians will finally emerge from their Temples, and tell their hidden secrets to the world!"

I, Psammetichus, had stood upon the Ennead. I had cut through the World Serpent, and looked into the Time outside Time. I had killed a God.

And now, I was about to take the corpse of my dead God, bottle it up, and sell it in the marketplace.

"Excuse me, brothers," I said in my flawless Koine, "but I am a native here, and I know the secrets of these things. They are not so complex as they appear."

"Who are you," said the first, "that speaks Greek so well? I have never met an Egyptian like you before."

"I received a true education at one of the Great Temples," I said. "That is how you find my diction to be so good."

"Then you know all of the secrets! Here, brothers, is a philosopher of the Egyptians themselves. Tell me then, oh philosopher, for we have been debating: who built this complex? Was he a man, or was he a God?"

I sighed, and gathered myself, pulling my cloak around me for warmth. To them it must have looked mysterious.

That's it, I thought. *That's my role in all this. Great.*

Psammetichus, your Kosmic tour-guide.

"Both," I said to the tourists, "a man and a God. Or a God, who came in the form of a man. And his name was Hermes Trismegistus."

APPENDIX

THE LAMENTATION OF RENPETNEFERET

I am a nameless voice. Hear me from the other side, and understand my calling. I have been forgotten.

To be forgotten is not an idle torment. The place I am now is like a purgatory. My soul has traveled on, but my memory lingers. I am the shadow cast by the consequences of my own actions. In this place, I exist as long as there is someone to remember me: as long as there is someone to make offerings to the ancestors, I continue. Maybe I only exist in name, but when the proper rituals are performed, I am given life again. And as long as my name, my image, survives in some form in the world, so will my

266

shadow here.

But when your name is neglected, when the offer-ings are not left before your shrine or the shrine of your family, your soul begins to degrade. When the monuments from your Kingdom crumble, your awareness is close to being snuffed out like a light. Like being held underneath the torrent of a raging river, where the current batters you senseless with-in an inch of total death.

But there are other ways to talk about time. I was not always a wandering, hungry ghost. Once I was a woman. Like you, I slept, ate, walked, talked, cried and defecated. I did not aspire to much. There was a time when all I wanted to be was a good wife, and I was willing to go to any end to fulfill that station: to do my duty. But that simple position in the world was not my fate. In the end, I found myself with an entire Kingdom at my disposal. In the end, I, an ordinary woman, found an entire Kingdom as my responsibility.

I do not think anyone understood how these events came to pass, even at the time. The turmoil that we faced, the destruction of everything we knew, and the chaos inside and outside our nation left us all nearly numb. Equally extraordinary were the great deeds that were done by those that rose to the occasion. I will tell you, I stood as silent witness to these deeds, at the eye of the storm — I was the nursemaid of these actions, and I held them in their deepest despair in the silent sobbing pangs of the night - and I do not understand them. I cannot understand them.

Where to begin? I was the wife to a prophet. As any woman in my position knows, being wife to a prophet is one of the worst things that can happen to anybody. It is hard. Yes, there are the sleepless nights, and there is the turmoil. But there is also the need to be unquestioning, because there is never time to question. So there is the blind faith which becomes synonymous with our love. Then there are the social functions, but the constant stress becomes rather automatic after a while. But the worst are the silent burdens that you must bear, as caretaker, mother, and handmaiden to a new epoch - these burdens are never named, never spoken of, never seen — and you must take them, nurture them as your own, because who would you be if you did not? What would any of us be?

Do not expect any thanks.

In your era, they call my prophet Imhotep. He was many things to many people. To me he was a good man. I never felt that I deserved any of this. He saw something in me that I could never see in myself. I never understood why he chose me. His vi-

268

sion extended so far to the future, sometimes I wonder if he saw where we are now. He supported me in a way no husband would ever do, except the most extraordinary. He believed in me, and he broke the most dangerous laws for me, for our whole family. Few men have ever believed in a woman the way he believed in me. He saw fit for me to be given instruction, an education.

You will remember him as the designer of the first pyramid, the architect who changed the world. Yes, he was this. But in our times he was so much more. We did not even understand the pyramid until after it happened. We were just trying to stay afloat. Imhotep was revered by the people as a man who performed miracles. In the face of the catastrophes — the chaos and famine — as a healer he shined like a light. His divinity became so self evident that eventually they had to recognize him. The King had to summon him to the court, a man whose position in the priesthood and among the people had already reached unheard-of fame.

Let me be clear, we were commoners. We were not nobility. My husband came from a long line of architects, and my father was a merchant. We were both from the suburbs of the city you Greeks call Memphis, but which we named for the beauty of its white walls. Inbu Hadju. I was common as muck. I had no sense of import, and only thought to support my husband as he took on a role in the priesthood. I knew he was extraordinary, and would do great things, but I did not know it would go this far. I did not realize, when we moved, that I would never be able to return to our home village. How could I have known? Commoners did not aspire to a higher standing in our society. We knew our role in life.

Of course, I was ambitious, and I knew what we were capable of. My husband was educated, and I knew that we deserved the best that we could get out of life. And I was an accomplished magician myself, I was a sorceress. Men and women knew the power of my speech, of my gaze. But there was not much respect for a mousey girl from the suburbs in those early days, when my husband was just beginning his work and his ascension. It was not the same by the end. We rose to heights unheard of, before or since. What happened to us happened only once in the entire history of the Kingdom. And it was beyond our petty human wills. Or at least mine.

The King named Imhotep to be the Regent of all of Egypt. The office of regent means that one is in charge of every practical affair in the entire country. In essence the regent runs the country, while the King maintains his symbolic function. Why did he do this? Understand that the King would never name any commoner to this position. Ever.

That is the extent of how extraordinary the events had become. Imhotep was a man in the process of becoming a God. He was on the path of the holy sage. He had just single-handedly saved the country from a famine and the people worshiped the ground he walked upon. They had no choice but to recognize him. It was self-evident that he was divine. How could they not?

They named him as 'Equal to the King.' In short he was held to be as divine as the King. Perhaps he was more divine, but everyone knew no one could commit that blasphemy. The outer form is different from the inner truth. And I was named Chief Handmaiden of the Queen's Ladies-in-Waiting. This was also a very important job. But it was largely a silent position, of holding things together for others.

The court of the King was very complicated. I was very much in over my head, in a sense, I think we all were. We were not prepared for the brutal games of the nobles. In the court, everyone holds multiple titles, and the complex interlinking of officials and courtesans means that it is very easy to inadvertently tread on someone's toes. There was a great deal of balancing one needed to do, between many different interests.

One way we handled it was by keeping secrets. We did not really know who we could trust. We

271

were better educated than some of the nobles, but it was not easy for us to move in those circles. Especially when some forces would rather we never stood in those shoes. There were plenty who would have liked to see us publicly discredited, and his divinity disgraced. So we fell back onto the one group we knew we could trust: family. The bonds of blood are not easily broken.

It was our family that took on most of the positions necessary - and as the chaos and near rebellion increased, those of us who were able stepped up to the occasion. This is one of the reasons why Imhotep had me learn Hieroglyphs, a forbidden art for a woman to learn at that time. I needed to be able to read and write so I could manage and notarize the documents we had to go through. And our family was running a country: there were never ending rolls of documents we had to handle. So my brother-in-law taught me in secret. They never found out.

I had great fun when I went to the market, and was able to read the tallying marks of the scribes. I never gave them enough so that they knew for sure I could read and write, I always played it dumb. Sooner or later every scribe knew, or suspected, and they learned to fear me. But they could never say for sure, and none would dare accuse me. With that and my mastery of the magical arts, the people knew I was a force to be reckoned with. A warrior-goddess of great esteem and fire, who slew with her gaze.

Knowing the sacred symbols changes you. You see deeper into the true nature of things. Your magic deepens too; you are able to see the meaning behind the words, and the hidden relations between all that is. He made me feel like a little girl. I was secretary to all his schemes. I felt like he was inscribing something within me, as if I was the scribal tablet and he was the stylus. I did not feel as though I understood what the message was I was meant to bear, or how to bear it. I am still unsure now.

In the midst of these great events, we began to build the funeral monument for Djoser. There was no plan. We never meant to build a pyramid. Pyramids did not exist yet, we did not know what we were inventing. All we knew was that these were crazy times, and that this monument had to be greater than any before it. At first we were building a simple mudbrick tomb. It became more.

But the only thing that is still standing is a Pyramid. That is the memory. A thousand tons of stone thrusting into the sky. The Pyramid is nothing. The Pyramid is just a husk.

The Pyramid is only the bones of memory. What use

273

is the Pyramid if there is no one there to worship it? What use are the altars of the ancestors if no one leaves them offerings?

Let me tell you what his invention means. The first innovation he made was that this should not be just a tomb where some offerings were laid once and a while. No, it was more than a tomb - it was a living temple, where the people were meant to go and make offerings well after the King was laid to rest. It was a marketplace, a forum, a place of life. It was no empty necropolis. And yes, sacrifices to the departed were also to be offered there — they would watch over us.

He had the vision of what it would be as we were building it. He fulfilled the fate of his family, as a long line of architects, through this vision. It was not just the King who ascended on this stairway, Imhotep built it too. It was his offering.

He had the vision — divinely inspired — without warning, to put another square tomb on top of the first one. And then another. The poor workmen had no idea what was going on. There was a lot of grumbling, and I often had to be there as a maternal figure to wipe noses and settle everyone's disputes. Imhotep was a man with a vision, he did not have time to pick up all the pieces. He was building a stairway to the stars. The workmen were not going to the stars. They needed bread. Although, to his credit in his off hours he was figuring out how the rest of the Kingdom would eat too...

He arranged mastaba on top of mastaba until the form of the monument became a perfectly shaped stairway to heaven. It was a ladder that the King's soul was meant to climb. It was a place of ascendance. In climbing that ladder, the death of the King was a sacrifice to link Earth and Heaven. He never set out to make that form. It was the consequence of all our lives, all our journeys together. In the complex he created columns modeled after bundled reeds of papyrus. These are the columns you Greeks stole when you later went to make your temples. King Djoser's monument was a microcosm of the otherworld. It was that world brought down here to Earth for the people to partake of. It was open to all.

But the rites for the funeral of the King were closed, though there were many mourners. And it was this ritual which made the link between Heaven and Earth — the King had died for his people. In mourning, the people's sins were redeemed.

It was a staircase to the stars. It was a way Imhotep showed to the world. And when he died, he took that stairway in his ascendance. From being in the presence of that, I ascended a bit too. In my passage through the afterlife, I, like many others I knew, followed this path to Heaven. But it is different being in Heaven on someone else's debt — my husband's. Although I stayed in that place for an eon of the world, eventually, I returned to Earth again. I failed a test and returned: I could not yet own my fate.

The world of Imhotep's vision was the background noise, the world of dream we returned to from our waking hours, our trials and tribulations. The world of the Gods. But in the daylight world, we had many dangers to overcome. To be honest, I do not think I would have survived the court were it not for the Queen. She took me under her wing, mentored me in the proper manners and rites, and taught me above all how to prevail against others who countered my will. She was like an elder sister to me, she took care of me, and I was endlessly devoted to her. We understood each other in the way of bosom friends. To her, I was not just a functionary. And I was put in the unenviable position of having to manage all of the handmaids when all of them wanted my head for getting the top office for nothing. There was hysteria, there were underhanded plots.

But with the Queen's gentle tutoring — and, I should add, her protection — I learned within a few years to master my position. I put down my enemies, it is true. But I never overstepped my bounds.

And the role of chief Lady-in-waiting mirrors the regent — you are the one who everyone in the court comes to, informally, when something is going wrong. You are the one who must handle all of their problems, their woes, their disputes — the ones that they cannot air in the public arena. And above all, you are their caretaker, their counselor, their friend. The bearer of their burdens. The silence of these burdens has nearly overcome me.

When I took up the position I was looked down upon as an upstart — yes, it is true — but later when I had proved myself, my relations with the girls changed. They became my compatriots, my closest friends. There are secrets women keep, like those passed from mother to daughter, which never touch the light of day. Laugh if you want to, but there was a power to what we did.

Our way of praising God was different than the men's, and we had a separate society from them. This was a way we had of preserving our power - as much as, in similar situations, then knew they must preserve theirs. And both men and women knew the consequences if they transgressed! That's how it was in the old world: there was respect, and with it, dignity.

When I trusted them, later, some of these girls

learned to write as well as me. They became the recorders of my visions, who would write my dreams after I incubated in the temple of the Goddess. I kept the ones I could trust close, and my secret visions, closer.

I was close with the Queen in a way I could never be close with my mother-in-law. I always felt like a fly on the wall, inferior, between her and Imhotep. They had a very tight bond. I felt as though I was an appendix, just some baggage that happened to be carried through. In the beginning, when we all lived together, it was quite hard for me. I did not feel that I had any role, or purpose to be there. I did not have a voice. In a sense, when we left, and I took on the duty I did, it was the best thing for me. I was able to relate to her better after that.

These were the hardest things for me: managing the handmaidens, and talking with my mother-in-law. The fact that I was a woman who was the secret secretary to an entire country, the fact that the entire court of the King relied on me to clean their dirty laundry and comfort their forbidden woes, that my husband had visions that led to spontaneously massive forms of architecture - these were very wearing, it is true, but they were nothing next to the simple woes all girls face in the transition from girlhood to womanhood. Yes, I was witness to a deep spiritual truth being realized. Yes, I saw a new epoch take form intimately, before my eyes. But when you are privy to such things, you find your perspective shifts. What stands out is the mundanity of it all, what is common. The true paths of life are simple, and walking them leads always to the same comforts and discomforts. Liberation is real, and it is a possibility, but it is a part of this simple, everyday pattern.

I find when I look back what I never said was how hard it was for me, to do all that work while never taking credit. But I also wonder how much of his motivation I ever understood. In truth, I often viewed him through the eyes of a child. His flashes of inspiration were so sudden, his vision was so deep, it often felt as though one was witnessing a God. I think I never appreciated — and still do not, fully — the extent to which he was making it up as he went along. He was taking each path that was meant for him, always fulfilling his line of duty. His vision informed him of his purpose from his already existing unity with God. I always attributed the deepest intentions to his actions. But this is probably inaccurate, and the forces that drove him were larger than any human intellect. It is hard, believe me, when you are in the presence of these forces.

So perhaps he could not know the consequences of the message he inscribed within me, a message I in part am giving to you now, or beginning to give. I do not think any of us knew the consequences of what we were doing. We were at the epicenter of the invention of so many things, that would reverberate through all the ages that followed. Not all of those things we invented were mere materials. And not all of their consequences were good.

But who can say of these things! None of us know the consequences of our actions. As we used to say in the old days, there is a little truth in a good wine. Be happy, because nothing gold can stay. No form will last forever. The moving finger writes, and having writ, moves on. My country does not survive. All that is left are its bones, the skeletons of monuments, and cadavers with no one to leave them offerings. Thank God your kind has not desecrated my grave: and you will never find it, nor my husband's. Our country has passed away! There are only shadows left. And to all the great Empires of the world, so too will be your fate. So drink wine, make merry — enjoy at least this time you have. It is the humblest service to God that you can offer.

Printed in Great Britain
by Amazon

41460842R00162